A CHRISTMAS EVE STOP

ALSO BY J.L. JARVIS

Waterfront Summers

(Can be read in any order)

The Cottage at Peregrine Cove

The House on Serenity Lake

Moonlight on Mariner's Bluff

Drake & Wilde Mysteries

(Reading Order)

1 Love in the Time of Pumpkins

2 Secrets in the Hollow

3 Shadow of the Horseman

Standalones

(Can be read in any order)

A Christmas Eve Stop

Christmas by Lamplight

A Kiss in the Rain

App-ily Ever After

Once Upon a Winter

The Red Rose

Highland Vow

Short Stories

(Can be read in any order)

Seasons of Love: A Short Story Collection

The Eleventh-Hour Pact

A Christmas Yarn

The Farmer and the Belle

Work-Crush Balance

Cedar Creek

(Can be read in any order)

Christmas at Cedar Creek

Snowstorm at Cedar Creek

Sunlight on Cedar Creek

Pine Harbor

1 Allison's Pine Harbor Summer

2 Evelyn's Pine Harbor Autumn

3 Lydia's Pine Harbor Christmas

Holiday House

(Can be read in any order)

The Christmas Cabin

The Winter Lodge

The Lighthouse

The Christmas Castle

The Beach House

The Christmas Tree Inn

The Holiday Hideaway

Highland Passage

For more information, visit jljarvis.com.

Get monthly book news at news.jljarvis.com.

A CHRISTMAS EVE STOP

J.L. JARVIS

A Christmas Eve Stop

ISBN (ebook) 978-1-942767-91-6
ISBN (paperback) 978-1-942767-92-3

Published by Bookbinder Press
bookbinderpress.com

CHAPTER ONE

ON CHRISTMAS EVE, trains carry two kinds of travelers: those rushing toward holiday celebrations and those quietly slipping away from them. But sometimes, when snow blurs the boundaries between what is and what might be, their journey may bring an unscheduled stop. It's a place that exists only in a moment of Christmas enchantment for those who might need it most.

LAURA QUINN MOVED through a crowded Penn Station with unhurried purpose, her caramel-colored hair tucked beneath a cream-colored knit hat. Her rolling carry-on made a soft rhythm against the polished floor, and she carried a leather messenger bag slung across her body. Unlike the frantic holiday travelers around her, she moved with the quiet assurance of someone who had carefully planned her escape.

She wore no Christmas sweater, no festive pins or holiday earrings—just a charcoal wool coat over a beige sweater and cream scarf, practical boots, and the particular expression of someone holding their composure like fine china. Not sad, precisely. Just contained.

As she approached the platform, she paused to check her ticket, brushing a melted snowflake from the screen of her phone. Business class was an indulgence she'd allowed herself this year. More space, more quiet, and complimentary beverages were small comforts that would make her journey to Boston easier. No one waited for her there. No one wondered where she was spending Christmas Eve. With two weeks off from teaching, winter break stretched ahead of her like a reprieve she desperately needed.

That was the point.

The train waited, gleaming silver with bright light spilling out from its windows. Laura boarded, found her reserved window seat facing forward, and settled in. The business-class car was nearly empty, with only a handful of other travelers spread throughout the car. She placed her messenger bag on her lap rather than stowing it overhead, a small barrier between herself and any potential seatmates.

She removed her gloves and gazed out at the platform where last-minute travelers hurried toward the train. That's when she saw him.

He moved with the fluid awareness of a man who had spent his life noticing things others missed. He was tall enough for his head to be inches away from the top of the doorway, with dark hair that was neither military-short nor fashionably long, just enough to show a hint of wave, slightly tousled from the wind. A shadow of stubble defined his jaw, emphasizing rather than softening its angles. He carried a single duffel bag with a soft-shell jacket slipped through the handles and wore a navy blue sweater over a button-down shirt and well-worn jeans.

Their eyes met for a mere heartbeat as he scanned the car. Something flickered across his face—recognition without knowledge. Laura felt an inexplicable sense that they'd been meant to see each other, although she was sure they'd never met.

He chose a diagonal seat from hers, across the aisle and one row ahead, facing hers. As he passed, she caught the faint scent of his cologne, something woodsy.

The train began to move, gliding away from the platform with gentle momentum. Through the windows, the lights of the station blurred into flashes of bright light against the dark tunnel walls. A family hurried down the aisle, parents juggling bags while shepherding two small children toward seats further back in the car. The younger child, a girl of perhaps four, clutched a well-loved plush snowman against her chest. The toy had clearly been through countless adventures—its orange carrot nose slightly bent, the green scarf fraying at the edges, and one coal button missing from its chest.

As the family passed Laura's row, the little girl's attention caught on something outside the window. Her grip loosened, and the snowman tumbled to the floor near Laura's feet. The family continued, the parents too focused on settling their older child to notice the loss.

Laura watched them continue down the aisle, then looked down at the forgotten toy. The snowman's embroidered smile seemed wistful in the overhead lighting. She recognized it immediately—the same style as the one from that animated film she'd watched countless times as a child, flying through the night sky with its young friend. The memory carried an unexpected weight.

She picked up the snowman, its fabric soft and worn beneath her fingers, and rose from her seat. The man across the aisle glanced up as she passed, and she felt his attention follow her progress down the car.

"Excuse me," Laura called gently to the parents, who were struggling to arrange their luggage in the overhead compartments. The mother turned, looking frazzled.

"I think someone dropped this," Laura said, holding up the snowman.

The mother's expression shifted to relief. "Oh, thank goodness. Ava, look." The child took the toy gratefully. "Thank you so much. You've just saved our Christmas."

"No problem." They exchanged smiles before Laura returned to her seat.

As she settled back in, she noticed the man watching her with an expression she couldn't quite read. It was not exactly judgment or interest, but perhaps a recognition of her small act of kindness. A fleeting glance passed between them before they both looked away, returning to their separate thoughts.

The conductor appeared, moving through the car in an unhurried routine, checking tickets and offering quiet greetings. There was something about him—an old-fashioned quality Laura couldn't quite pinpoint. His uniform was modern and pressed, but something in his expression seemed to belong to an earlier era. When he reached Laura, she held out her phone.

"Boston?" he asked, though he could clearly see her destination.

"Yes."

He scanned her e-ticket. "It should be a smooth journey if the weather holds off." He moved on to the man across the aisle, repeating the process with the same quiet efficiency.

The train gathered speed as it emerged from the tunnel, and the city gave way to the suburbs. House windows glowed with Christmas lights, trees twinkling in living rooms where families gathered. Laura pulled her book from her messenger bag—a paperback mystery novel, its spine already cracked from being opened and closed during her commute. Something engaging enough to occupy her mind but not so compelling that she couldn't set it aside if sleep came.

The train pulled into Stamford, and the car door burst open with a rush of cold air. A man stumbled through, clearly having run to catch the train at the last possible moment. His face was flushed—whether from running or from the office holiday party Laura guessed he'd just left was debatable. His tie hung loose, his suit jacket was askew, and he carried the aggressive cheer of someone who'd had just enough drinks to think everyone wanted to be his friend.

"Made it!" he announced to no one in particular, scanning the car with bright eyes. His gaze landed on the empty seat beside Laura's. He dropped into the seat, bringing with him a cloud of cologne mixed with bourbon and the manic energy of forced holiday spirit.

"Heading home for Christmas?" he asked immediately, not waiting for an answer. "Me too! Well, heading to Boston first, then my sister's place. You know how it is—family, obligations, the whole nine yards. But hey, it's Christmas, right? Season of joy and all that!"

Laura offered a polite smile, the kind she'd perfected over years of practice. "Mm."

"Nice? It's fantastic! I mean, sure, my ex-wife will be there with her new boyfriend—Gary, can you believe that name? Gary. Sounds like an accountant, which he is, actually." The man laughed, a sound too loud for the quiet car. "But hey, I'm not bitter. It's Christmas! Peace on earth, goodwill toward Gary, right?"

Laura turned toward the window and lifted her book slightly. It was meant as a signal, but the man either didn't notice or didn't care.

"Are you traveling alone? Me too! Well, obviously. But you know what? Sometimes, alone is better. No one to answer to, no one to disappoint." His voice carried a sharp edge beneath the cheer. "Though Christmas alone is rough, am I right? That's why I'm going to my sister's. Can't face the apartment alone on Christmas. Too quiet. You know?"

Laura made no response, her eyes fixed on her book, though she wasn't reading a word.

"Oh, you're reading! Don't let me stop you. I'll just..." But he didn't stop. "Actually, I can never concentrate on trains. Too much going on, you know? All these people, all with their own stories. Like you—what's your story? Let me guess—visiting family? Boyfriend waiting in Boston?"

She turned a page, saying nothing.

"Not a talker, huh? That's okay. I can talk enough for both of us. My ex-wife used to say that. Said I never knew when to shut up. Of course, she's with Gary now, so what does she know?"

The man across the aisle—the one who'd boarded just after her—shifted in his seat. Laura caught the movement in her peripheral vision as he turned slightly toward them.

"Listen," the drunk man continued, his hand gesturing wildly, nearly knocking Laura's book from her hands. "Christmas is about connections, right? Human connections. Not books. We should be talking and sharing. That's what my therapist says, anyway. Share more. Connect more. Though he also says I should drink less, so what does he know?" Another too-loud laugh.

Laura's fingers tightened on her book. She angled her body further toward the window, practically pressing against it.

"You know what your problem is?" the man asked, and something in his tone shifted, becoming more aggressive. "People like you, you're all closed off, reading your books, acting like you're too good to talk to someone. It's Christmas Eve, for crying out loud!"

That's when the man from across the aisle stood. He moved with deliberate calm, the kind of controlled movement that suggested he could move much faster if needed. He stepped into the aisle and addressed the drunk man with a tone that was conversational yet carried an unmistakable authority.

"Excuse me, but you're in my seat. I just went to stretch my legs."

The man blinked up at him, processing slowly. "Your seat? But I thought—"

"Easy mistake." The stranger's voice remained friendly, but his presence—the way he positioned his body, the steady gaze—communicated something else entirely. "It happens all the time. Your ticket probably shows a different car."

"I... maybe?" The man fumbled for his ticket, squinting at it. During his distraction, the stranger caught Laura's eye for just a moment. The message was clear: Play along.

"Yeah, see?" The stranger continued, though he hadn't actually looked at the ticket. "Next car back. Better seats there anyway, closer to the café car."

"Oh. Oh, right." The drunk man stood unsteadily. "Sorry about that. Merry Christmas!"

"You too," the stranger replied, maintaining his position until the man had stumbled through to the next car. Only then did he turn to Laura.

"Thank you," she said quietly.

He nodded once and, after a moment's hesitation, returned to his original seat.

He pulled out his phone immediately and began scrolling. Laura returned to her book, starting the chapter over since she hadn't absorbed a word while the drunk man was talking.

The only sounds now were the pulsating thump of the train on the tracks, the distant murmur of conversations from elsewhere in the car, and the occasional rustle when one of them shifted position. Each seemed acutely aware of the other—the way strangers are when forced into proximity—but neither acknowledged it.

Outside, the snow was falling harder. She noticed him glance at the window, a slight frown crossing his features. The flakes had grown thick, swirling in the lights of the passing towns and reducing visibility to mere yards.

The car attendant appeared as they neared New Haven, pushing a small cart down the aisle. "Beverages? Coffee, tea, or soft drinks?"

"Coffee, please," Laura said, grateful for the prospect of warmth and caffeine.

The stranger looked up from his phone. "Same."

The car attendant smiled apologetically. "Let me check if I have enough in this carafe." He poured one cup and frowned at the nearly empty container. "I'll need to go back for a fresh pot. I'll just be a few minutes."

He handed Laura her coffee and moved on. She wrapped her hands around the warm cup and inhaled the rich scent. The man beside her returned to his phone, though she noticed his jaw tighten slightly. It was such a small thing, wanting coffee on a cold night without having to wait.

She almost offered him hers, but the words died before they formed. They'd established their mutual silence. To break it now would be to acknowledge... something.

The car attendant returned, looking genuinely distressed. "I'm so sorry, sir. The coffee machine has completely broken down. Some kind of electrical issue. I can offer you tea, hot chocolate, or juice."

"Tea's fine," the man said, his tone neutral.

But Laura caught the slight slump of his shoulders, the way his thumb moved restlessly across his phone screen, although he didn't actually seem to be reading anymore. She understood that sometimes appearing occupied provided an illusion of privacy when everything else felt vulnerable.

The train began to slow for New Haven. Passengers gathered their belongings, and families bundled children back into coats. The business-class car emptied considerably, with only a handful of travelers continuing toward Boston. When the train pulled away from the station, Laura realized they were the only two left in their section of the car.

The snow was becoming a real storm now. Even through the train's solid windows, they could hear the wind picking up. The lights of passing towns became fewer and farther between until there was nothing but darkness and the hypnotic swirl of white in the train's lights.

The man had given up pretending to read his phone and instead watched the storm through the window. There was something tense in his posture, the alertness of someone tracking potential danger.

Laura found herself watching it too—the way the wind drove the snow almost horizontally at times and the way ice was beginning to form on the window edges. She gave up reading and pretended to stare out the window, but her eyes were on the stranger's reflection in the glass.

The train's rhythm had become hypnotic. Other sounds faded until there was only the steady clack of wheels on rails, the whisper of air through the vents, and her own measured breathing.

She became aware of small things: the way he held his phone with his right hand, a scar along his forearm visible where his sleeve had ridden up, and the controlled stillness of someone used to waiting and watching. He never fidgeted or shifted unnecessarily. Even his breathing seemed deliberate.

He was aware of her, too. She could tell from the slight turn of his head when she moved. They were two people working hard to maintain their solitude despite sitting too close to ignore.

The storm intensified. The train rocked slightly in a particularly strong gust, and both of them tensed. Outside, it was a complete whiteout now, the darkness and snow combining into an impenetrable wall. She noticed him checking his watch, probably calculating how far behind schedule the weather might put them.

Then the train's cadence changed.

It was subtle at first—a slight deceleration that could have been a curve in the tracks. But it continued with the wheels slowing their percussion against the rails. The man straightened, and his hand went still on his phone. Laura looked up from her book.

They were slowing more definitely now, but according to the route map on the wall, there were no stops scheduled for at least thirty more minutes. She glanced at him and found him turning to look toward the front of the car with that alert tension back in his shoulders.

The deceleration continued, steady and deliberate —not the sharp braking of an emergency, but the measured slowing of an intended stop. Outside, the forest pressed close to the tracks, with trees heavy from snow creating a tunnel of white. Through the storm, there was nothing to see except shadows and swirling snow.

The train slowed further. The man leaned toward the window and peered intently. Laura found herself doing the same on her side, though neither commented on their parallel actions.

Then, through the driving snow, lights began to appear. Unlike the usual harsh fluorescence of train stations, these appeared warmer through the haze of the snow. The glow barely penetrated the storm but instead created soft halos of light in the swirling white.

As the train continued to slow, shadows of structures began to take shape—a train platform, and beyond it, the suggestion of buildings. The architecture looked old and charming, what little Laura could see of it, with a slate-shingled roof and gabled windows barely visible.

The train eased to a stop with a gentle sigh of brakes.

Silence.

No announcement came over the intercom. The train simply sat there, humming quietly, while outside the storm raged and warm lights glowed through the snow.

Laura and the man exchanged a glance. Outside the window sat a small depot with red brick, cream-colored trim, and a steep roof heavy with snow. Arched windows glowed warmly from within, and ornate iron brackets held lights that swayed slightly in the wind. The platform stretched alongside, covered by a Victorian-style canopy supported by decorative iron pillars. Snow had gathered in the scrollwork, softening the edges. It looked like something from a model train set—perfectly preserved and completely unexpected between the familiar Connecticut towns.

The train sat silent, waiting.

CHAPTER TWO

THE CONDUCTOR APPEARED in the doorway. "Folks, we're making a brief stop here. The weather's getting rough ahead—dispatch wants us to wait it out while the tracks are cleared. It shouldn't be more than an hour or so. There's a coffee shop in the station if anyone wants to stretch their legs, but stay close and listen for updates."

He moved on to the next car. Laura glanced at the man beside her. He was already standing and pulling on his jacket, still not making eye contact or acknowledging their proximity of the last hour. He moved past her and down the aisle.

She waited until he'd exited before gathering her things. She pulled on her coat, working the buttons slowly, then lifted her messenger bag from the seat. The car emptied quickly, with most passengers seeming eager to escape the confined space, if only for a short while.

She felt the cold immediately when she stepped

onto the platform. Not the bitter, aggressive wind of the city, but clean, damp coastal air scented with pine and wood smoke. Snow fell steadily in large flakes that drifted rather than drove.

The depot building drew her forward. Through the windows, she could see warm yellow light, people moving about, and the promise of coffee. She pushed through the heavy wooden door.

Inside was a small waiting room that looked as though it hadn't been updated in decades, with wooden benches worn smooth, a potbellied stove in the corner—decorative now—and radiators doing the real work. Old railway posters covered the walls. A small coffee counter had been set up along one wall, too modern to be original but trying to fit in. Above it, a hand-lettered sign read "The Depot Café."

The stranger was already there, second in line. Laura hesitated, then joined the queue several people behind him. The space was too small for the crowd from the train, creating an intimate bustle. She could hear him order—"Just black"—his voice carrying the same controlled tone from the train.

When her turn came, the young woman behind the counter smiled. "I've got dark roast or a hazelnut blend."

"Dark roast is fine."

While the girl poured, Laura became aware that the stranger hadn't left. He stood near the window, looking out at something beyond the depot. She followed his gaze and saw a cluster of lights through the snow that looked warm and inviting—the suggestion of a town square, maybe, or a main street.

She paid, took the warm cup, and went to another window—one that gave a similar view but kept a distance between them.

Through the falling snow, she could make out what looked like a town green, trees strung with lights, and the outline of buildings that seemed to glow from within. It was like looking at a snow globe—that same perfect, contained world that couldn't quite be real.

The waiting room had largely emptied as passengers returned to the train or stepped outside for fresh air. But she stayed at the window, and he stayed at his, both looking out at the lights of the town.

A couple pushed through the door, laughing and shaking snow from their coats.

Laura saw the stranger's shoulders tense slightly, the way someone does when they're about to move. He set his empty cup on the windowsill and walked to the door, pushing out into the snow.

She waited long enough so that it wouldn't seem like she was following him, and then she did the same.

Outside, the snow had created a hushed quality, muffling sounds and softening edges. The lights she'd seen through the window were clearer now—definitely a town square, maybe a five-minute walk from the depot. She could hear music, faint but unmistakable, voices raised in song.

The stranger was walking in that direction, hands in his pockets, shoulders hunched against the snow, but not hurrying. She let him get farther ahead, then found herself walking the same path—not following him, but curious... about the town. She had twenty minutes to kill, after all.

The path from the depot was shoveled but already coated with fresh snow. It wound through a small stand of pines, their branches heavy and white, then opened onto something that made her stop.

A perfect New England town square spread before her, like so many Christmas cards she'd opened, or the holiday movies she used to love watching at this time of year. A massive tree towered over the square, where people moved through the snow with purpose.

Except for the stranger. He'd stopped, Laura noticed. He stood at the edge of the square, separate from the crowds, simply watching. She stayed where she was, yards away, and took in the scene.

Its picturesque nostalgia could have felt false or cloying, but somehow it didn't. Maybe it was the way the lights were all soft white instead of glaring colors, or how the decorations looked worn and loved, as if they'd been pulled out of attics year after year. But it was the carol she heard being sung, "O Come All Ye Faithful," unamplified instead of being blasted through speakers, that harkened to a time all but lost.

The stranger moved first, walking slowly along the edge of the square and keeping to the shadows outside the pools of lamplight. After a moment, Laura did the same, choosing the opposite direction. They traced the perimeter, observing but not venturing toward the center.

Her eyes kept being drawn to the glow of windows, the groups of people laughing, and the children playing in the snow. And occasionally, through the swirl of flakes and bodies, she'd catch sight of him—a dark figure against the lights, as separate as she was, and as watchful.

She paused at a storefront—a bookshop with vintage Christmas editions displayed in the window. When she glanced up, she could see his reflection in the glass, standing on the opposite side of the square, looking at something she couldn't see. Their eyes met in the reflection for just a moment before she looked away, focusing intently on the book spines.

From the gazebo, "Good King Wenceslas" carried on the wind as voices rose and fell with more enthusiasm than skill. A family passed her, the parents swinging a small child between them, all three bundled in matching scarves. The child's laughter rang out, clear as bells.

She moved on to the next window, an antique shop with a collection of old ornaments, some of which looked like they were from as far back as the 1940s. The glass baubles and tinsel stars looked like the kind her grandmother might have had. She touched her fingers to the cold glass without thinking, then pulled them back, leaving brief prints that fogged and disappeared.

The stranger had moved too, she noticed. He stood near the fountain now, still separate from everyone and still watching. Something about his posture and the set of his shoulders suggested someone used to standing guard. But guarding against what, or whom, she couldn't guess.

A vendor near the gazebo was selling hot chocolate and candy canes. The small crowd around the carolers had grown, some joining in, others just listening. It was organic, unforced—not so much a performance as a gathering.

Laura wandered closer to the center, drawn there despite herself. She stopped at a bench, not sitting but standing beside it, and watched the carolers. They'd moved on to "Silent Night" now, and even the imperfect voices couldn't diminish the song's simple beauty.

That's when she noticed the inn.

It stood at the corner of the square, three stories of Victorian elegance. Painted soft yellow with white trim, every window glowed with warm light. Wide porches wrapped around two levels, both decorated with simple greenery and white lights. The ground floor seemed to house some kind of restaurant. She could see figures moving behind fogged windows, the suggestion of a fire, and the warm bustle of people gathering.

Without conscious decision, she began walking toward it for a look and to warm up for a minute. The train would leave soon, so she wouldn't linger long.

She'd made it halfway across the square when she realized the stranger was walking in the same direction, approaching from his side. They would reach the inn's entrance at almost the same moment if they kept their current pace.

Laura slowed deliberately, pausing to examine a shop window she had no interest in. She would let him go in first before she reached the door. But when she looked up, he'd stopped too. He was standing near the inn's entrance and studying the menu posted by the door with apparent concentration.

They stood frozen in their separate spots for a long moment, each seeming to wait for the other to move. Finally, a group of laughing friends pushed past him and through the inn's door, breaking the spell. He followed them in.

Laura slipped her hands into her pockets and waited. Her fingers were getting cold, so she slipped on her gloves. The snow was beginning to stick to her coat. A couple emerged from the inn, bringing with them a brief burst of warmth and the sound of conversation. She walked to the door, pulled it open, and stepped inside.

The vestibule was small, designed to keep the cold from rushing into the main building. A second door, this one with etched glass panels showing holly and ivy patterns, led to the lobby, where soft jazz arrangements of carols were playing. The smell of real food—not just bar snacks—made her stomach rumble, reminding her she'd skipped lunch.

The lobby was everything a Victorian inn should be —all dark wood, Persian rugs, and a grandfather clock ticking in the corner. A fire crackled in a massive fireplace, and the air smelled of lemon oil. A few other people sat in chairs near the fire, reading or talking in low voices.

Warm light glowed through a frosted window on one side of the lobby, where a painted sign read "Evergreen Books & Tea" in elegant script, with a smaller inscription beneath: "Est. 1892." To the left of the door, a handwritten card proclaimed, "Hot cider, warm soup, and good books. What else does anyone need?"

She pushed open the heavy door, and a brass bell chimed overhead. Heat rolled out from the black potbellied stove in the corner. It was smaller than she'd expected—more nook than bookstore—with floor-to-ceiling shelves creating intimate alcoves throughout the space. A long oak counter ran along one wall, where a woman in a cable-knit cardigan was pulling something from a small oven.

It was also wonderfully, overwhelmingly full.

Every wingback chair was occupied. The window seats held readers curled with books and steaming mugs. A chess game occupied the table by the stove, where two elderly men studied the board with the intensity of generals preparing for battle. In a nook marked "Poetry Alcove," a young couple sat close enough that their knees touched while they pretended to read. What looked like a book club had commandeered the entire children's section, where a handful of teens discussed with enough animation to carry: "But if she knew about the letters, why didn't she just—"

The only open seats were three stools at the tea counter.

Laura scanned the room without meaning to, looking for him. There he was—already at the counter, on the furthest stool, with his back to the room and absorbed in a book.

The smart thing would be to leave and go back to

the train early, where she could wait in the warm, quiet car.

Instead, she walked to the counter, choosing the furthest stool from him, and sat with one stool between them. Not much, but something.

The woman behind the counter looked up from arranging pastries and beamed. She was perhaps sixty, with silver hair in a loose bun and reading glasses on a beaded chain around her neck.

"Oh, good, you made it! I wondered if you'd gotten lost. The directions I gave weren't the clearest." She was already reaching for a mug. "The usual?"

Laura blinked. "I'm sorry?"

"Oh!" The woman's hand flew to her chest. "Oh my goodness, I thought you were— We're expecting someone, and in this snow, everyone looks the same all bundled up. You're not my niece from Hartford, are you?"

"No, I'm just... passing through."

"On the train? Of course. We've had a steady stream tonight. Let me guess—delayed by the storm?" At Laura's nod, she continued, "Third delay this week. I swear, between the weather and the holidays... Well, what can I get you? The mulled cider is my grandmother's recipe, and I just pulled a fresh batch of cranberry scones from the oven."

"Cider sounds perfect. And maybe something more substantial?"

"The pot pies are gone, I'm afraid—those went fast. But I have butternut squash soup with grilled cheese on homemade sourdough. Real comfort food. The soup comes in these lovely bread bowls from the bakery next door."

"That sounds wonderful."

The woman bustled away, and Laura let herself settle slightly. This was fine. This was what she'd do in any city—find a quiet spot, have dinner alone, and disappear into the atmosphere. The fact that he was here too was just a coincidence. In a small town with limited options, they both sought the same thing—a warm, comfortable place to pass the time.

She pulled off her gloves and unwound her scarf. The warmth of the room was almost overwhelming after the cold. By the time she'd tucked her gloves into her pockets, the woman was placing a glass mug of cider in front of her, steam curling up with the scent of cinnamon and cloves.

"The soup will be just a minute. I'm Mae, by the way. I own this place, for better or worse." She gestured at the controlled chaos of the bookshop. "Twenty-seven years now."

"Laura."

"Well, Laura, if you need anything—" Mae stopped mid-sentence, looking past her. "Oh, there she is! Susan!"

The door chimed, and a young woman rushed in, shaking snow from her coat. "Aunt Mae, I'm so sorry I'm late! The roads are terrible, and Tom's truck wouldn't start, and—"

"It's fine, honey. I already gave your stool away, but we'll find you a spot." Mae scanned the shop. "Actually... hmm."

Laura started to stand. "I can move—"

"Oh, no, it's just a silly tradition. Since she was little, she's always had a favorite spot on the end." Mae was looking between Laura and the end of the counter where the stranger sat. "Sir? I hate to ask, but would you mind scooting down one? My niece just arrived, and if we could squeeze her in at the end there..."

He looked up from his book, and his eyes found Laura's for just a moment. "Of course."

He gathered his book and his mug of tea and moved to the middle stool. Right next to hers.

"Perfect!" Mae beamed. "Susan, honey, have a seat. I'll get you something hot."

And suddenly, Laura was sitting close enough to catch the scent of his jacket, still carrying traces of snow and pine. Close enough to see the title of his book, *A Farewell to Arms*.

"Good book," she said, then immediately wanted to take it back. They'd maintained careful silence on the train. Why break it now?

He glanced at her. "Have you read it?"

"In college."

Mae returned with Laura's soup—a round of sourdough hollowed out and filled with velvety butternut squash soup topped with a swirl of cream. The grilled cheese was cut into triangles, the bread golden and crispy, with cheese oozing from the edges.

Mae moved away to help her niece, and Laura focused on her soup despite being far too aware of every movement, lest she touch the stranger beside her. She could see him in her peripheral vision, the way he turned pages carefully and lifted his mug without looking away from his book.

The bell chimed again. A woman entered with two small children, both in snow boots that squeaked on the wooden floor.

"Mrs. Garcia!" Mae called out. "Story time was this afternoon, honey."

"I know, but they insisted on coming in to say good night to the books." The woman looked apologetic. "Five minutes?"

"Of course. You know where the children's section is."

The children, a boy and a girl of approximately four and six years old, dashed toward the back, their mother trailing behind with an indulgent smile. The little girl reminded Laura of one of her students, Sophie, who loved books about dragons and always begged to be the line leader.

"You know what I love about used books?" a quiet voice said beside her.

She turned. He was still looking at his book, but he'd spoken to her.

"The margin notes," he continued. "Someone underlined this whole passage about second chances and put three exclamation points next to it."

"That must be some passage," she said.

"Or maybe they just really liked exclamation points." He tilted the book so she could see. "When I saw her, I was in love with her. Everything turned over inside of me."

Laura said, "The previous owner was young and in love. Just a guess." They shared a smile.

She found herself really looking at him for the first time. In the warm light of the bookshop, she could see that the green in his eyes had flecks of gold. There was a faint scar through his left eyebrow. He had the kind of face that would age well—good bones, as her mother would say.

"I always wonder about the people who leave notes," she said. "Like they're having a conversation with someone they'll never meet."

"Maybe they are."

She held his gaze for a moment, something shifting in the air between them.

"I'm guessing," she said, looking away. "It was one of those two in the poetry section."

His mouth twitched—almost a smile. "The ones who've been whispering over the same book for twenty minutes?"

"While holding hands."

He said, "Very impractical for page-turning."

"Maybe it's a really compelling page."

"Must be." A smile bloomed on his face as he looked into her eyes. It took her by surprise, so much so that she couldn't look away. Or breathe.

It was the longest exchange they'd had, and it felt like they'd crossed over to something—not friendship exactly, or even warmth, but... acknowledgment. Of shared space. Of the absurdity of maintaining elaborate distances after spending a day so close together.

When she finally glanced down, she noticed some

pages had slipped from his grasp, revealing an underlined passage that read, "The world breaks every one
and afterward many are strong at the broken places."

She didn't realize she was frowning until he
followed her gaze to the passage. Their eyes met and
held, neither speaking.

The children raced past again, the little boy
carrying a picture book about trains. "Mama, can we get
this one? Please? It has a red caboose!"

"You have six train books already, Xander."

"But not this one!"

Laura nearly smiled despite lingering thoughts of
the Hemingway passage. For children, and perhaps for
adults as well, there could be an almost sacred connection to a particular book that made it different from all
others by some invisible quality.

He said, "You work with children." It wasn't a
question.

"How did you know?"

"The way you're watching them, like you're recognizing more than observing."

She took a sip of cider to avoid responding. He was
too perceptive. It made her nervous.

"The train one is different," he said suddenly, loud
enough for the mother to hear. "That's the one where
the train gets to choose its own tracks at the end. It's
about agency, really. In most train books, the trains just
follow predetermined routes."

The little boy's eyes went wide. "See, Mama? It is
different!"

The mother gave him a grateful look. "All right, Xander. But just the one."

The boy clutched the book to his chest and ran back to show his sister. Laura stared at the stranger. "How could you possibly know that?"

"I don't. But now the boy gets his book, and he'll believe it's about choosing your own tracks. Maybe that matters more than what it's actually about."

"That's very..."

"Dishonest?"

"I was going to say kind."

He went back to his book, but she caught something in his expression—surprise, maybe, at his own intervention.

The chess players made a decisive move—she heard the piece click on the board and one of them say, "Check." The book club was debating whether the protagonist deserved forgiveness. The couple in the poetry section had progressed to a longing gaze.

Mae returned to refill Laura's cider. "The snow's really coming down now. They're saying it might be the worst storm in decades." She glanced between them with barely concealed curiosity. "Good thing you both found somewhere warm to wait."

Through the window, Laura could barely see across the street. The snow had created a wall of white, turning the world into a snow globe someone wouldn't stop shaking. It was beautiful and terrifying at once—the kind of storm that erased boundaries and made shelter feel smaller while the whole world felt larger.

"My grandmother used to say storms like this were

nature's way of making people slow down," Mae continued. "Forcing us to stay put, to actually see where we are instead of always rushing to where we're going."

She moved away to help another customer, leaving them in silence again. But it felt different now. Companionable, almost. They were just two people sharing a counter during a storm.

The bell over the door chimed again. The conductor from their train entered, stamping snow from his boots. "Anyone here for the 5:35 to Boston?"

Several hands raised, including Laura's and the stranger's.

"We're looking at another hour, at least. Maybe two. The tracks on the way to New London are completely blocked. I'd tell you to get comfortable, but it seems like you already figured that out." He touched his cap and left.

Laura ordered another cider. He got a second cup of tea. The children left with their mother, the boy clutching his train book. The chess players barely noticed while new people entered, shook off snow, and marveled at how bad the weather was.

"Another hour or two?" he asked suddenly.

She looked at him hopelessly. "Yeah."

He nodded toward the chess players by the stove. "How about a game?"

That took her by surprise. "What sort of game?"

"We make up stories about the people we see. But we can only observe, not listen."

"Still, that seems invasive."

"More invasive than what we're already doing? We

can't help watching people, and it's not invasive if we're making it up."

"I suppose so."

With a glint in his eyes, he said, "The truth is, we're probably making them more interesting than they really are."

She considered. It was a way to pass the time that didn't require real conversation or real sharing. "Fine. You start."

"Those two playing chess—friends or enemies?"

Laura studied them—the way they hunched over the board with identical postures, how one kept touching a particular pawn without moving it, and the other's small smile of satisfaction. "Friends, but there's an undercurrent of rivalry."

"I'm intrigued."

Laura thought for a moment. "It happened 40 years ago over something stupid that became the most important thing in their lives."

Without hesitation, he added, "A woman."

"Yes. They both loved her, but she married... someone else entirely. And moved out of state."

"Where?"

"California. They've been replaying that loss through their chess games ever since."

"Dark."

"The truth sometimes is." She nodded toward the poetry section. "Those two. What's their story?"

He observed the man and woman, both wearing wedding rings. "Coworkers. They work for the county. Office jobs. They're married, but not to each other.

Every Thursday, they come here and 'happen' to run into each other."

"They never buy any poetry," Laura added. "They just hold the same book and talk quietly about... not poetry."

"Dramatic."

"Heartbreaking."

A burst of noise came from the children's section, where Mae had set up a semicircle of pillows. Three generations had arranged themselves for an ad hoc story time—a grandmother beaming, three overstimulated children, and two parents pretending to be more enthusiastic than exhausted.

"The grandmother there," he said, "drove two hours to be here. Sees the grandkids once a month. This is her time."

"That teen girl off to the side? She's secretly recording it," Laura observed. "For TikTok. But she'll watch it later when no one's around and love that her little brother still does the voices."

"The dad's feigning interest, but look how he keeps turning back and hiding how he's checking his phone."

Laura raised an eyebrow. "Another woman or work?"

"Work. He's buried—way in over his head. There are rumors of layoffs at work, and he's afraid he's getting laid off. He's right, but he doesn't know it yet."

They went quiet, aware they'd ventured somewhere too real.

"What about us?" Laura asked, then immediately

regretted it. "I mean, what would someone observing us think?"

He considered. "Two people helping each other pass the time."

"That's exactly what we are."

"Not exactly," he said quietly. "That's what we're choosing to be."

Mae suddenly appeared beside them, cocking her head like she was listening to something distant. "There's your PA announcement," she said, pointing toward the fogged window.

They looked at each other, and then they were moving—grabbing coats, scarves, and gloves, racing for the door. The bell chimed frantically as they burst out into the storm.

The snow was knee deep now as the wind drove it sideways. Laura immediately lost her footing, and his hand caught her elbow, steadying her. They ran—or tried to run—through the drifts, following the sound of the whistle.

The train was there with its lights glowing through the storm. They stumbled aboard, breathless, with legs covered in snow.

"Made it," the conductor said, then frowned at his radio as it crackled to life. He held up a hand, listening. His expression shifted from welcome to resignation.

"What is it?" Laura's voice came out sharper than she intended.

"Just got word from dispatch. Sorry, folks. We're not going anywhere tonight. There's signal trouble past New London and a fallen tree beyond that. They've got crews working, but with this storm..." He shook his head. "Nothing's moving until at least tomorrow afternoon, maybe longer."

The train car suddenly felt too small. Snow melted off their coats, creating puddles at their feet.

"So we're stuck here," the stranger said as though he couldn't believe it.

"Afraid so. The station's already arranging accommodations. They are setting up cots at the high school gym, but since you are hearing this first, you might make it to the inn in time to get a room there." The conductor's radio crackled again. "I wouldn't waste any time. They're saying it's the biggest storm to hit Connecticut in twenty years."

They stood frozen for a moment, processing the news. Then, without speaking, they climbed back down to the platform.

The wind had picked up, erasing their footprints from minutes before. Laura stumbled again, but this time his hand found her elbow and stayed there.

They weren't friends. They weren't even acquaintances, really. But they were no longer quite strangers either. And now, it seemed, they were both trapped in Evergreen Junction.

CHAPTER THREE

THE WALK back from the station was quiet except for the crunch of their boots through deepening snow. By unspoken agreement, they'd stayed together through the worst of the drifts, made it back to the inn, and secured two rooms, but the rooms weren't ready for check-in, so they left their luggage and headed back out to explore.

The square looked different in the storm—transformed from the quaint New England postcard Laura had glimpsed earlier into something from a snow globe that had been gently shaken and set down to settle. The massive pine at the center seemed taller now, its thousands of small white lights blurred by falling snow into amber halos. No colored bulbs, no tinsel, no mechanical reindeer. Just lights nestled among the branches like captured stars.

They stopped at the edge of the green, their breath misting in clouds that mingled briefly before the wind tore them apart. The warmth of Mae's bookshop, the cider, and the invented stories all felt like something that had happened to other people. Their alliance seemed to have dissolved.

"Well," the stranger said, the first word either had spoken since leaving the train.

"Well," Laura agreed.

She had developed a particular awareness of his presence beside her, this stranger with whom she'd been stranded for hours. The smart thing would be to stick together to face it. After all, there was safety in numbers. Or was that strength? And yet, without another word or acknowledgment of what they'd shared or of what lay ahead, he moved left around the square, and she went right.

The town green spread in a perfect rectangle, bordered by storefronts that looked like they'd been there since the railroad first came through. Simple wreaths hung from lampposts that lined the town square. Victorian facades with their gingerbread trim intact, painted in deep reds, forest greens, and cream. Each window held a single electric candle, and pine boughs framed the doorways.

Laura walked slowly, as if in a dream. The snow fell like feathers, soft and silent, muffling the world. After the earlier bustle of Penn Station—the pushing crowds, the electronic boards, the blaring announcements—this felt like stepping through a veil into another time. Lamps cast a soft glow on their surroundings, plumes of wood smoke drifted upward from the chimneys, and bells faintly jingled from somewhere out of sight.

A gazebo anchored the far end of the green, where

warm white lights illuminated the delicate scrollwork of the white-painted wood from within. A small group had gathered there—not performers, just townspeople by the look of them. Different ages, different voices. They were discussing something, sheet music was being passed around, and there was gentle laughter at someone's suggestion.

Then they began to sing.

"Hark! The herald angels sing..."

The voices weren't perfect. An older man's baritone wavered slightly. A woman sang a quarter-tone flat. But something about the imperfection made it more charming. Like a memory of Christmas from childhood, when everything still held magic.

Laura walked toward the sound, drawn despite herself. The melody was so familiar she could feel it in her bones. Her kindergarten class had sung this at their holiday concert just two days ago. Twenty-five five-year-olds in their best holiday clothes, half of them forgetting the words, two crying from stage fright, and one waving frantically at his grandmother throughout the entire song.

She'd stood at the side of the auditorium's small stage, mouthing the words along with them, ready to prompt if they forgot. Afterwards, the parents had swarmed the stage, scooping up their children, praising them, and taking photos. She'd helped zip coats, tie scarves, and find lost mittens. "Merry Christmas, Miss Quinn!" they'd called as they left. "See you next year!"

Then she'd driven home alone to her empty apartment, where she'd watched an old Christmas film rather than hear the silence.

A vendor had set up near the gazebo. "Hot cider! Warm yourself up!"

The smell of cinnamon and cloves drifted toward her, and Laura found herself approaching.

"Just a small one," she said, fishing for her wallet.

"Small, medium, or large—they're all the same price tonight," the man said with a wink. "Christmas Eve special."

He handed her a paper cup, steam rising from the surface. She wrapped her hands around its warmth and breathed in the scent. The first sip tasted the way Christmas was supposed to taste, before she'd started avoiding it.

GABE LAWSON WATCHED her from across the square, not intentionally, just aware. It was a habit, really—knowing where people were, what they were doing, and cataloging exits and entrances. Seventeen years on the force didn't just switch off because you weren't carrying a badge anymore.

She stood by the cider vendor, holding her cup like she was trying to absorb its warmth. The gray coat she wore was well-made but not new. He'd noticed some pilling in the tea shop. She wore stylish but practical boots, the kind people wore in the city when they weren't relying on taxis and rideshares. There was no jewelry that he'd noticed, no wedding ring. The messenger bag she carried was worn leather.

She worked with children, so teacher was the obvious guess. Or librarian. It had to be something that involved caring for others. She had that particular patience to her manner, the kind that came from dealing with chaos while maintaining calm.

Not that it was any of his business. He was just killing time until the train left, and she was just another stranger doing the same.

A child ran past him suddenly, maybe six years old, clutching what looked like homemade gingerbread. The boy's mother followed, laughing, calling for him to slow down. The boy spun in a circle, arms out, head tilted back to catch snowflakes on his tongue, and the cookie flew from his hand.

It landed in the snow directly between Gabe's bench and where Laura stood at the fountain.

They both moved at the same instant. Both took one step forward, and both stopped when they realized the other had moved. Their eyes met across the fallen cookie—a moment of mutual awareness, mutual hesitation.

The mother caught up, scooping up both boy and cookie with practiced ease. "Brayden, you need to be more careful!"

"The gingerbread man ran away!" the boy protested, struggling in her arms.

Gabe found himself responding without thinking. "Well, he didn't get very far, did he?"

The boy's eyes went wide, and then he giggled. "He got eaten by a fox!"

"See? He should have kept running."

The mother smiled at him. She turned to Laura. "Sorry if he bothered you."

"Not at all," Laura said softly. She was almost smiling, Gabe noticed. Almost, but not quite.

The mother and her son moved on. Gabe returned to his bench while Laura turned and walked toward the shops on the far side of the square. They were back in their separate orbits, two satellites carefully maintaining distance around the gravity of the town square.

THE SNOW WAS FALLING HARDER NOW. Fat flakes stuck to her coat and her hair, turning the world soft at the edges. Laura had finished her cider but held onto the empty cup. The carolers had shifted to a new song, their voices carrying across the square with bell-like clarity.

"Jingle bells, jingle bells, jingle all the way..."

A cheerful song. Children were clapping along near the gazebo, their mitten-clad hands muffled but enthusiastic. Some adults had joined in, swaying slightly, cups of hot drinks steaming in their hands.

"Oh, what fun it is to ride in a one-horse open sleigh..."

Laura found herself walking closer, drawn by the circle of warmth and light they created. The scene was perfect—too perfect, like a painting in a museum. The kind of Christmas that existed in movies and memories, but never in real life.

"Jingle bells, jingle bells, jingle all the way..."

The chorus came around again, voices rising. Children laughed at the "HEY!" at the end, shouting it with glee.

"Oh, what fun it is to ride in a one-horse open sleigh!"

She walked on, following a path that curved around the square. The shops gave way to the entrance of what looked like a park or walking trail. She could see benches along the path lined with lampposts, creating pools of light on the snow. Everything was bathed in a dreamy glow.

That's when she saw them.

Two figures flanked the entrance to the park path. Her brain took a moment to process what they were. Life-size wooden nutcrackers at least six feet tall, painted in bright reds and blues with gold trim, were positioned as if guarding the entrance. Their mouths were carved in perpetual grins with bared white teeth. Black-painted eyes stared as if taking in everything.

Laura's feet stopped moving. The empty cup slipped from her fingers and landed silently in the snow.

The nutcrackers looked just like the ones she remembered.

"Jingle bells, jingle bells..."

The carol drifted across the square, but now it sounded different. Slower. The lyrics—"laughing all the way"—took on an edge.

Her heart kicked hard against her ribs as it started to race.

The nutcrackers' painted eyes seemed to track her. Their grins stretched wider in the shifting light from the lampposts. Those weren't smiles. They were bared teeth. Threatening. Warning.

"Laughing all the way... HA HA HA..."

The children's laughter from the gazebo carried on the wind, but it sounded wrong now. Mocking. The Christmas Market, a year ago yesterday. The entrance had been guarded by nutcrackers like these. The same height. The same colorful paint and the same dead eyes that had watched it all happen.

"Jingle bells, jingle bells..."

She'd been looking at handmade ornaments. Silver bells, actually. Little silver bells with etched angels. The vendor, an elderly woman with kind eyes, had been wrapping one in tissue paper.

"...laughing all the way..."

The crowd had been singing. Different carols then, but the same oblivious joy.

"HA HA HA..."

The laughter in the song wasn't joyful anymore. It was cruel. It knew what had happened. It was laughing at her for thinking she could recover, for thinking she could have a normal Christmas ever again.

Someone bumped into her from behind. Hard. A man walking fast, talking on his phone. His hand grabbed her elbow to steady himself as he passed. The touch sent electricity through her arm, the wrong kind of electricity. From fear.

The nutcrackers' eyes followed her now. She couldn't seem to evade them. Their painted pupils tracked her as she stumbled backward. Their grins were getting wider. The rifles in their wooden hands looked ready to lift, to aim, to—

"Jingle bells, jingle bells, jingle all the way..."

The ground wasn't solid anymore. It rolled like a ship's deck. The lights from the lampposts smeared into long streams. Her chest was too tight, like someone had wrapped bands around it and was pulling them tighter with each breath she tried to take.

Air. She needed air. But the air was full of snow and that horrible laughing—"HA HA HA"—and the nutcrackers were leaning forward now, about to step off their pedestals, about to come for her with those wooden hands and painted smiles and—

Her shoulder hit something solid. A lamppost. The metal was ice-cold through her coat, real in a way nothing else felt. She grabbed it with both hands and held on like it was the only thing keeping her from floating away or falling through the earth.

"Breathe."

The voice came from beside her. Low. Calm. Just that one word.

She turned her head. The stranger from the train stood a few feet away, not too close, with his hands in his pockets. His eyes were on the nutcrackers, not her.

"Can't—" The word came out strangled.

"Yes, you can." Still calm, but now looking at her. "In through your nose. Hold it. Out through your mouth."

She tried, but the air wouldn't come. The band around her chest was too tight.

He moved then, just slightly—enough to position himself between her and the nutcrackers, blocking her view of them. There he stood, solid and still, his body forming a wall between her and the painted eyes.

"In through your nose," he said again. He demonstrated, exaggerating so she could see his chest rise. "Hold. Out through your mouth."

She mimicked him. The first breath barely made it past her throat. The second was slightly deeper. By the fifth, the band had loosened enough for real air to get through.

"Jingle bells, jingle bells..."

She flinched at the chorus coming around again.

"It's just noise," he said quietly. "Just people singing. Nothing more."

But the laughter—the "HA HA HA"—

"Look at the ground," he said. "Count the snowflakes landing on your boots."

It was an impossible task. The snowflakes landed and melted immediately. But trying to count them meant looking down, meant focusing on something small and specific instead of the enormity of her panic.

One. Two. Three melting into the leather. Four. Five. Six.

Her breathing steadied. The ground solidified under her feet. The lamppost felt like just a lamppost again, not a life raft.

When she looked up, he'd stepped back and given her space. The nutcrackers were still there, but they were just wooden decorations again. Gaudy, oversized, but harmless. The carolers had moved on to "Silent Night," and the manic laughter was gone.

He studied her for a moment, that same assessing look she'd caught on the train. Whatever he saw seemed to satisfy him that she was stable. He nodded once—a small, decisive movement—and turned to walk away.

"Thank you," she called after him.

He paused but didn't turn around. "There's a tavern on the corner."

Then he kept walking, hands still in his pockets, disappearing into the snow.

Laura stayed by the lamppost for another few minutes, making sure her legs would hold her. The panic had passed, leaving her feeling hollowed out and exhausted. The square still looked like a Christmas card, but now its edges were torn, and the picture was slightly off center.

She waited until she was sure he was gone, then she pushed off from the lamppost, tested her legs, and found them steady enough. The nutcrackers still flanked the park entrance, but they'd lost their power now, reduced to what they'd always been—painted wood and nothing more.

The tavern stood at the corner of the square, three stories of Victorian dignity painted a soft yellow with white trim. Every window glowed warmly. Through the glass of the ground floor, she could see movement and hear the muffled sound of conversation and laughter.

Normal sounds. Safe sounds.

She walked toward them.

Inside, it smelled of old wood and beer. The murmur of conversations seemed to hover along with the clink of glasses and an echo of jukebox music.

The choice of a tavern was perfect. The anonymity of a dimly lit, crowded bar was just what she needed right now. The dark wood paneling had aged to a warm patina. A long bar of polished mahogany with a brass footrail stretched the length of one wall, while round tables with mismatched chairs were scattered throughout. At the far end, a fireplace warmed the room.

What she hadn't hoped for was that the bar would be packed. Every table was full. Groups of friends laughed over beer, couples shared plates of food, and what looked like an office party had relocated here from somewhere else. The noise level was perfect—loud enough for privacy, not so loud you had to shout.

She scanned the bar. Most of the stools were taken, but there were a few empty spots. Three in a row at the far end where he sat, and two scattered singles in the middle—one wedged between rowdy groups, another right by the service station where the bartender was busily mixing drinks while servers rushed past.

He sat at the very end of the bar in the back of the room, nursing what looked like whiskey. Two empty stools sat beside him like a buffer zone he'd deliberately created.

Laura hesitated. She could take one of the middle seats and cope with the crowd. She could leave and find somewhere else. But where? And why should she? She just needed a warm place to wait for the train.

She made her way through the crowd and chose the middle stool with an empty stool on either side of her, giving her a reasonable distance from anyone. Neutral territory.

She'd barely settled when the door burst open, bringing a rush of cold air and a couple.

"Sandy!" One of them called to the bartender. "Tell me you've got room for us!"

The bartender—a woman about Laura's age with auburn hair pulled into a messy bun—surveyed the crowd with practiced efficiency. Her eyes landed on the empty stools beside Laura. "Mind scooting down, hon?"

Before Laura could respond, the pair was already moving and claiming the space with the cheerful aggression of the slightly drunk. As Laura slid down one stool and sat directly beside him, her coat brushed his arm.

"Sorry," she said quietly.

"No problem," he said, avoiding her gaze, but she noticed his jaw tighten slightly.

The office party swirled around them, with people pressing close, talking over one another. Someone's elbow kept bumping against Laura's side, and others were reaching past her for drinks. They were surrounded, hemmed in by Christmas cheer, body heat, and noise.

The bartender appeared in front of them, looking harried but maintaining her smile. "What can I get you folks?"

"Irish coffee, please," Laura said, her stomach still

full from the soup but wanting something warm, something to hold.

"Another whiskey," he said.

"You two together?" the bartender asked, already pulling out one check pad.

"No," they said in unison, too quickly.

The bartender glanced between them—two people pressed together by circumstance, rigid with the effort of maintaining boundaries that had already been erased by sheer proximity—and shrugged. "Separate checks, then. Though you might be the only two in here not celebrating something."

She moved away to handle the office party's complex order of shots and festive cocktails. Laura tried to shift slightly away, but there was nowhere to go. Someone had hung their coat on the back of her stool, and the person on her other side kept gesturing wildly with their drink.

"This is ridiculous," she muttered.

"We could leave," he said, still not looking at her.

"And go where? Everywhere's probably like this tonight."

"Fair point."

Her Irish coffee arrived in a glass mug, the cream floating perfectly on top. She took it and inhaled the whiskey and coffee scent, more for comfort than any desire to drink it. Her stomach was still pleasantly full from Mae's soup, but the warmth of the mug felt necessary, grounding.

She became aware of how still he'd gone beside her, that particular kind of stillness she recognized from her own bad moments—when you were working hard to look normal while something inside was unraveling. Without thinking, she shifted slightly on her stool, closing just a fraction of the distance between them. Not touching. Just... there. Close enough that she could feel the warmth from his body. Close enough to notice a thin scar across his right knuckles and that he smelled faintly of the outdoors, pine, and snow.

"The twenty minutes are up," someone from the office party announced. "Where's our table?"

The bartender began herding them toward the back, and suddenly the bar felt cavernous. The stools on either side of them were now empty. They could move apart now and reclaim their distance, but neither of them moved.

"We could spread out," she said, but made no motion to shift.

"We could," he agreed, also staying put.

They sat there, no longer pressed together by necessity but still close enough that their arms almost touched on the bar. Around them, the tavern had grown quiet. The fire crackled. Someone fed quarters into the old jukebox, and Bing Crosby started crooning "White Christmas."

"This is absurd," Laura said finally. "We keep ending up..." She gestured vaguely at the small space between them.

He turned to look at her then. In the warm light of the bar, his eyes were more green than she'd realized. "We could just... stop pretending we're not sitting together."

"We could," she agreed.

The bartender returned, noticing their nearly empty glasses. "Another round?"

Laura looked at her half-finished Irish coffee. "Actually, just water for me."

"The same," Gabe said, though his whiskey was gone.

The bartender's face fell slightly—water wasn't good for tips on Christmas Eve. "We've got a killer bread pudding tonight. Big enough to share, if you're interested."

Laura caught Gabe's eye. They'd both just eaten at Mae's, but the bartender looked hopeful, and it was Christmas Eve, and maybe sharing dessert wasn't the worst idea.

"Bread pudding sounds good," he said, looking at Laura for confirmation.

"With two spoons," she agreed.

The bartender smiled like she'd known all along they were together but just hadn't admitted it yet. "Coming right up."

Minutes later, the bread pudding arrived, fragrant with cinnamon and vanilla, drenched in bourbon sauce that pooled around the edges. It was too much for one person, especially after a full dinner, but perfect for sharing while the snow fell outside and the fire crackled within.

"I'm Laura," she said suddenly.

He looked at her and hesitated, as if sharing names was a line he wasn't sure they should cross.

"Gabe."

They were just names, but it felt like they'd entered new territory. Laura said, "It almost feels as though this"—she gestured vaguely at the space between them, the shared dessert, the snow falling beyond the windows—"being here... isn't real."

He seemed to understand. Some things were too fragile for the real world. "It's as real as anything else around here," he said quietly.

She nodded and felt a sense of relief mixed with an ache that was never too far away.

They ate slowly, managing the dessert between them. Outside, the snow was relentless, covering the world in white and making everything feel new and strange.

"I wonder if it would be worth stopping by the train depot for a status update," Laura said, checking the time.

"It wouldn't hurt. It would be optimistic, but why not?" But neither moved to get up.

They sat there, two strangers who'd shared too many spaces in one evening, no longer pretending they weren't aware of every breath, every movement, or every small closing of the distance between them.

CHAPTER FOUR

THE BARTENDER HAD ALREADY CLEARED their plate when Gabe pulled out his wallet. Laura reached for her purse, but he waved her off.

"We'll settle up later," he said, leaving cash on the polished wood.

They pulled on their coats as the temporary ease they'd found over dessert seemed to dissipate.

"Do you think we should check the depot for updates?" she said, though neither of them moved immediately. The warm glow of the tavern windows behind them made the storm ahead seem even more forbidding.

"Yeah." He turned up his collar. "We can always hope."

Outside, the snow had picked up considerably, thick flakes driving sideways in gusts that made Laura pull her scarf higher. They walked without speaking, their footsteps muffled by the accumulating snow. The festive lights of the square blurred through the falling flakes, creating halos of amber and white. A few hardy souls still moved between buildings, but most of the town had retreated indoors.

The depot, when they reached it, was dark except for a single bulb over the entrance. Their boots echoed on the wooden platform as they stomped off the snow. Gabe tried the main door, which was, thankfully, open, and they stepped into the waiting room.

It offered shelter but little warmth. The decorative potbelly stove in the corner was unlit, and the radiators along the walls were cold to the touch. Behind the ticket counter, the office sat dark and empty.

Laura approached the ticket window, her breath fogging the glass. A handwritten sign taped to the inside read, "Next departure: December 26 at 6:50 a.m."

"December twenty-sixth," she said flatly.

"If the weather clears." Gabe had pulled out his phone, squinting at the screen. "Still no service."

"Of course not."

They stood in the cold waiting room, both reluctant to acknowledge what this meant. Two more days, at a minimum. The reality of their situation settled over them, silent and out of their control.

Laura turned to face Gabe. In the depot's dim emergency lighting, his features looked carved from the shadows. "So we're stuck here. In a town with no signal, that's not on the route, and with no train for two days at the earliest."

"Looks that way."

The practical implications started stacking up in her mind. "Well, it's back to the inn, then."

They stepped back into the storm. If anything, it had intensified while they were inside. The wind drove snow horizontally, and visibility had dropped to mere feet. Laura pulled her hat lower and wrapped her scarf across her face, but the cold still found every gap in her clothing.

They retraced their path toward the town square, fighting the wind with each step. Laura's boots weren't handling the ice very well, and she slipped. Gabe's hand shot out and caught her elbow, steadying her until she found her footing.

"Thanks," she gasped through her scarf.

He didn't let go immediately. "Stay close. I can barely see."

They walked closer together after that, using each other as anchors against the wind. The path that had seemed charming earlier now felt treacherous. Tree branches heavy with snow hung low over the walkway. Drifts had formed against buildings, sculpted by the wind into strange shapes.

When they finally emerged onto the square, it looked transformed. The festive lights swayed wildly on their wires, some already dark. The gazebo where carolers had sung was now just a white mound. Even the massive tree at the center seemed diminished, its lights barely visible through the driving snow.

The inn's yellow paint glowed ghostly in the storm, but every window radiated warm light. Laura had never been so grateful to see a building in her life.

They fought their way up the porch steps. Gabe

pulled open the heavy door, and they stumbled inside, bringing a gust of snow with them.

The warmth hit like a physical force. They'd entered a small vestibule with hooks for coats and a bench for removing snowy boots. Through an inner door with etched glass panels, she could see the inn's main lobby.

Gabe was already shaking snow from his jacket and stamping his feet. His hair was white with snow, and his cheeks were windburned red. Laura caught sight of her own reflection in a small mirror on the wall and winced —she looked like she'd been in a fight in a windstorm and lost.

"Ready?" he asked.

She wasn't sure what she was supposed to be ready for, but she nodded anyway. They pushed through the inner door.

Behind a polished wooden desk, an older woman looked up from her ledger. She had silver hair pinned in an elegant bun and a demeanor that suggested both competence and kindness. Her expression didn't show surprise at their snow-covered appearance—only a knowing sort of welcome.

"Good evening," she said warmly. "Caught by the storm, I see."

"We reserved rooms earlier, but they weren't ready before," Laura said, then felt foolish stating the obvious.

"Of course." She stepped into a back room and emerged with their luggage. "You'll need to check in." The innkeeper handed them each a pen and a paper to fill out and made some entries in her ledger. "I'm

Mrs. Wright, by the way. Welcome to the Evergreen Inn."

Laura finished her form first, despite her hand still feeling stiff from the cold.

Mrs. Wright produced two keys. "Rooms seven and nine, second floor. Breakfast is served at eight in the dining room, and we put out some coffee and pastries at six for early risers." She paused, studying them with sharp but not unkind eyes. "The storm is supposed to get worse before it improves. You made the right choice coming in."

"Thank you," Laura said, taking her key. The metal was cold in her palm, and the wooden tag read "7" in neat brass numbers.

"If you need anything, ring the desk."

They climbed a narrow staircase that creaked under their weight. The second-floor hallway was dim and cozy, with floral wallpaper and wall sconces that cast pools of amber light. Laura's room was the first door on the right, and Gabe's was the second door down from hers.

They stood in the hallway, suddenly awkward. The train's delay had given them a shared purpose, but now that they'd secured shelter, the reality of the situation settled over them. They were stranded together in a strange town. They would be here for two nights, possibly longer.

"I should—" Laura started.

"Yeah," Gabe said. "Get warm. Dry off."

"Right." Laura turned her key over in her hands. "Goodnight, Gabe."

"Goodnight, Laura."

She let herself into room seven and closed the door, leaning against it. The room was small but charming—a double bed with a thick quilt, a wardrobe, and a small desk beneath a window. The radiator clanked and hissed, filling the space with welcome warmth.

Through the window, snow continued to fall until the town square was barely visible through the curtain of white. Tomorrow morning felt very far away.

Somewhere down the hall, she wondered if Gabe was standing at his own window, watching the same storm, thinking the same thoughts.

CHAPTER FIVE

LAURA COULDN'T SLEEP, and she couldn't stay in that small room another minute. The walls pressed closer with each passing moment, and the silence was too loud —filled with all the things she was trying not to think about. The clock on the nightstand showed nearly midnight, but she felt wide awake, her body still humming with the strange energy of this place.

She got dressed and made her way downstairs. Each creak of the inn's narrow staircase sounded sharp in the quiet night. The lobby was dimly lit and empty. Most guests had already retired for the night and, unlike her, were probably sleeping.

Except for one. A figure stood near the window, looking out at the square. Gabe. His hands were in his pockets, his shoulders relaxed, but with that particular stillness he had that made him seem always alert. He turned at the sound of her footsteps, and for a moment, they just looked at each other.

"Couldn't sleep?" he asked.

"Something like that." She moved closer to the window, maintaining a distance between them. Through the glass, the square glowed under lamplight, snow still falling steadily. "Strange day."

"That's one word for it."

They stood there, both looking out at the transformed world beyond the glass, while unspoken questions seemed to hang in the air.

"There's a fire in the parlor," he said after a moment. "I was going to..." He gestured vaguely.

"Oh. I don't want to intrude—"

"You wouldn't be." He paused. "Unless you'd rather be alone."

She should have said yes, she'd rather be alone. That was what she'd planned when she got on that train that morning—distance and solitude in a place where nothing could hurt. But something about this place, this night, made her usual defenses feel pointless.

"A fire sounds nice," she heard herself say.

The parlor was just off the lobby and down a short hallway, a small room she hadn't noticed before. Dark wood paneling gleamed in the low light, built-in bookshelves lined the walls, and two worn leather chairs flanked a fireplace where logs crackled softly. The room smelled of old paper and wood smoke, with the faint sweetness of pine from the garland draped along the mantel.

Gabe moved to one of the chairs, and Laura took the other. The leather was soft with age, conforming immediately to her body. The fire popped gently, sending shadows dancing across the walls.

"It's strange being here—in this town," she said, needing to fill the silence. "I didn't know this place existed."

"It was here when we needed to find it."

She looked at him then, really looked. The firelight cast half his face in shadow, highlighting the sharp angle of his jaw and the controlled way he held himself even in repose. There was something familiar about him, something that tugged at the edge of her memory.

"I keep feeling like I know you," she admitted. "But that's impossible."

He was quiet for a long moment, staring into the fire. When he spoke, his voice was lower and rougher. "Maybe not as impossible as you think."

Something in his tone made her pulse quicken. "What do you mean?"

He stood abruptly and moved to a small cabinet in the corner. "I need a drink for this conversation. You?"

"Yes."

He produced two glasses of whiskey from the bar, which operated on an honor system, with a ledger to charge to the room. He held out a glass that glowed amber in the firelight, and their fingers brushed. The contact sent an unexpected frisson through her.

He settled back in his chair, took a drink, and then turned the glass slowly. The silence stretched until Laura tried to think of something to say—anything—to ease the tension.

"Jingle Bells," he said suddenly.

"What?"

"Earlier today. At the square. When you had the panic attack. It was triggered by that song."

Laura's hand tightened on her glass. "How did you—"

"Because I recognize the signs. Because I have the same trigger." He took a sip of whiskey, and she noticed his left hand remained in one position, slightly curled. "The Bryant Park Winter Village. Last year. December twenty-third."

The room seemed to tilt. Laura set her glass down, afraid she might drop it. "You were there?"

"I was."

Her mind raced, trying to place him in the chaos of that day. The crowds, the music, the sudden eruption of screams and gunfire. She'd been looking at ornaments when the world exploded into terror.

"I don't remember seeing you," she said, though something nagged at her, some detail trying to surface.

"You were wearing a red scarf," he said quietly. "With fringe on the ends."

Laura's breath caught. She'd loved that cashmere scarf, an indulgent gift to herself weeks before.

"Blood," she whispered. "It was covered in blood."

"Mine," Gabe said simply. "You used it to stop the bleeding after I was shot."

The memory slammed into her with physical force. A man on the ground, blood spreading across the snow, her hands pressing desperately against the wound, the warmth leaving his body, and her voice breaking as she repeated over and over—

"Stay with me," she breathed. "That's what I kept saying. Stay with me."

"You saved my life."

"No, I just—I pressed on the wound and talked. Anyone would have—"

"No one else did." His voice was firm. "Everyone else ran, but you stayed."

Laura stood, unable to sit still with these memories flooding back. She moved to the fireplace, gripping the mantel. "You're the cop. The one who tried to stop him."

"Failed to stop him."

"You were shot protecting people." She turned to face him. "I watched you tackle him even though you knew he was armed. You gave people time to escape."

"Not enough time. People still died."

"But more would have without you." The pieces were falling into place now—his damaged hand, the way he held himself, the hypervigilance. "The bullet went through your hand."

He stood and examined his left hand in the firelight. The scar was a starburst of pale tissue. "Nerve damage. Three surgeries, four months of physical therapy. I can't hold a weapon properly anymore, so it ended my career. I had to take a disability retirement."

"I'm so sorry."

"For what? You're the reason I'm alive to complain about it."

They stood facing each other in the small room, the weight of the shared memory heavy between them. Laura recalled everything now—the terror, the blood, and the desperate minutes before the paramedics arrived. She remembered the shooter. His eyes had locked onto hers for an instant, and she was stunned by how young he had looked. What was a boy doing on the street, shooting at people?

"I tried to find you," she admitted. "After. I called hospitals, but privacy laws—"

"I know. I tried to find you, too." He set down his glass and took a step toward her, but he still maintained his distance. "I went back to the market after it reopened. I asked the vendors if they remembered a woman with a red scarf. No one did."

"Why?"

"To thank you. Because you stayed." He met her eyes. "In seventeen years on the job, I saw terrible things. Most people run from danger. It's a normal reaction—human nature, the drive for survival. But you knelt in the snow next to a stranger and refused to let me die alone."

"Maybe I was just too scared to move."

"No." His voice carried absolute certainty. "You were scared, but you stayed anyway. That's not the same thing."

Laura felt tears prick at her eyes. The weight of the past year—the nightmares, the isolation, the constant fear—suddenly felt crushing. "I haven't been able to wear red since. I don't handle crowds well. I can't even listen to Christmas music without—" Her voice broke.

"I know." And he did know. She could see it in his eyes, the same shadows she carried.

"Is that why you were on the train? Running from Christmas?"

"Running from everything," he admitted. "A friend's cabin in Maine, in the middle of nowhere. No decorations, no music, no memories."

"I was going to Boston, then driving to an empty beach town." She laughed, but it was futile. "We were both running to nothing."

"And ended up here instead."

"In a place that shouldn't exist."

"Maybe it exists just for people like us," Gabe said. "People who need... something. Healing. Hope? I don't know."

The fire crackled, sending sparks up the chimney. Outside, the snow continued to fall, insulating them from the world. Laura wrapped her arms around herself, suddenly cold despite the warmth of the room.

"I dream about it," she said quietly. "The shooting. I try to hold your hand still while pressing on the wound. You kept trying to get up."

"I had to stop him."

"You nearly died trying."

"I would have, without you."

They stood there, two people bound by the worst day of their lives, finding each other in an impossible place on Christmas Eve. The coincidence of it—or the fate of it—felt too large to comprehend.

"All year," Laura said, "I've felt like a ghost. Going through the motions. Teaching my kids, planning lessons, pretending everything was normal when nothing felt normal anymore."

"Same. Except without the teaching. Just... existing. The early retirement gave me too much time. I've been stuck. It's like I've been waiting for something, without knowing what."

Laura knew the feeling. When she would run out of things to keep her busy, she found herself in a sort of limbo, unsure of what to do next and yet feeling the past creeping back. "Maybe we were waiting for this. For answers."

He looked straight at her. "Or for each other."

As the words hung between them, something in his expression relaxed, as if his defenses were crumbling. She recognized it because she felt it too.

It was too much. Too sudden. The recognition, the shared trauma, the pull she felt toward him—it was overwhelming.

"I should go." She gestured toward the door. "It's late."

"Wait." He took a step toward her, then stopped. "I know this is a lot. And it's late. But would you... Mind taking a walk with me? Just around the square. I don't think I can go back to that small room right now."

Laura understood. After everything they'd just revealed, she felt on edge. She had too much nervous energy to return to that small room. "Yes. A walk sounds good."

They collected their coats and headed outside. The snow had stopped, and the night was clear and still. Stars wheeled overhead, brighter than Laura had ever seen them. The square was empty except for the two of them and the soft glow of lamplight.

They walked without speaking at first. Six more inches of snow had fallen since the sidewalk had been cleared. Everything in the town felt suspended, held in a moment between one breath and the next. Porch lights glowed with warm light, but the streets themselves were deserted.

"Thank you," Gabe said finally. "For that day. For staying when you could have run. For giving me something to hold onto when everything else was a nightmare."

"Thank you for being here now. For understanding." She paused. "I haven't talked about that day with anyone. Not really. My friends tried to be supportive, but they didn't know what to say. How could they?"

"They weren't there."

"And you were."

They reached the gazebo at the center of the square and stopped. The decorations still hung from its rafters, swaying gently in the night breeze. Gabe leaned against one of the posts, and Laura stood near him, both looking out at the sleeping town.

"Do you think we would have found each other?" Laura asked. "If not for this place?"

"I don't know. The odds were against it."

"But somehow we did."

"Here we are."

He turned to look at her, and in the lamplight, his eyes were dark and serious. "I'm glad we are. Here, I mean. That the train stopped. All of it."

"Me too," she whispered.

The space between them felt charged and alive with hope. Laura was intensely aware of every detail—the way his breath clouded in the cold air, the slight stubble on his jaw, the way he held himself with that careful control that was starting to slip.

He lifted his hand, the damaged one, and hesitated. Then slowly, giving her time to move away if she wanted, he reached up and tucked a loose strand of hair behind her ear. His fingers were cold against her cheek, but his touch was gentle.

"Laura," he said, and her name in his voice sounded like a question.

She didn't know what the question was, but she found herself leaning into his touch, answering it anyway. His other hand came up to frame her face, and she could feel him trembling slightly—whether from the cold or something else, she couldn't tell.

The moment stretched between them, crystalline and fragile. There was want in his eyes, but also hesitation. They'd only really known each other for hours. The connection felt profound, but was it real or just the product of shared trauma and this strange, magical place?

"Maybe we should go back," she said softly, though she didn't move.

He nodded, agreeing, but his hands remained where they were, cradling her face like something precious.

Then the church bells began to chime midnight, breaking the spell. Twelve clear notes rang across the sleeping town. Gabe's hands dropped, and they stepped apart, both breathing a little harder than the cold warranted.

"It's Christmas," Laura said unnecessarily.

"Yeah."

Their walk back to the inn was charged with awareness and the weight of the moment they'd shared. At the stairs, they paused.

"Goodnight, Laura."

"Goodnight, Gabe."

He lifted her hand and pressed a kiss to her knuckles—a gesture that should have felt old-fashioned but instead felt like a declaration of the feelings they weren't ready to acknowledge out loud. Then he walked to his room and disappeared inside.

Laura stood in her doorway for a long moment, her hand still warm where he'd kissed it. Then she went inside and fell onto her bed fully clothed, too overwhelmed to do anything but lie there and process what had just happened.

They'd found each other. After a year of searching, after giving up hope, they'd found each other in this impossible place. And the recognition hadn't broken them; it had connected them in a way that felt inevitable yet a little terrifying.

Laura pressed her fingers to her lips, feeling the echo of a kiss that hadn't happened but somehow hovered in the space between them.

She couldn't begin to know what tomorrow would bring. But tonight, she had this: the knowledge that she wasn't alone in her trauma. Someone else understood. The same man she had saved had just saved her in return, simply by being there and recognizing her. They were no longer alone because they shared something neither would have wished for. It had brought them together.

CHAPTER SIX

Voices drifted up from the square—not quiet early morning start-of-a-new-day voices, but lively ones laughing and scraping something across the cobblestone walkway. She reluctantly opened her eyes and then went to the window, where she found a town square that was transformed.

The snow-covered expanse was now filling up with booths, with lights strung between them. Interspersed with the booths, tables lay covered with red and green checkered cloths. An increasing array of handmade goods was being displayed. Someone was testing a sound system, playing instrumental carols at a volume that carried but didn't overwhelm.

Laura dressed quickly in jeans and her warmest sweater, then made her way downstairs. The dining room was nearly empty except for Mrs. Wright, who was covering dishes with kitchen towels.

"Oh, good, you're up," the innkeeper said brightly. "I was hoping for someone to help me carry these out.

The town decided last night—since we're all snowed in anyway, why not proceed with our Christmas market? Everyone's bringing something to sell or share."

"That's... nice," Laura said. The word "market" made her tense slightly, but she pushed the feeling down.

"Your friend is already outside helping set up tables." Mrs. Wright's eyes twinkled at the word "friend," but she didn't elaborate. "Would you mind taking this banana bread? My friend Yolanda is already there. Tell her I'll be out with the cookies in a minute."

Laura accepted the covered basket, still warm from the oven. Outside, the morning air was crisp but not bitter, and the snow was bright from the sun. The transformation of the square was even more impressive up close. What had started as a few tables was becoming a proper market. Three rows of booths formed a U-shape around the central tree, leaving the middle open for foot traffic.

Laura spotted Gabe immediately. He was helping an elderly man secure a canopy over a table of carved wooden toys. His movement was easy and natural, and when he laughed at something the man said, the sound carried across the square. It warmed Laura's heart to see him so relaxed and unguarded.

He noticed her and raised a hand in greeting, but he continued with his task. Laura brought the bread to the bake sale table, where Yolanda was arranging items with military precision.

Yolanda glanced up and, spying the bread, said, "Perfect timing! Let's put that right here in front. Mrs.

Wright's banana bread always sells first." Yolanda beamed at her. "Isn't this wonderful? We haven't had a proper Christmas market in years, but the storm's given us the perfect excuse."

More townspeople arrived, carrying boxes and bags. A woman set up a table of knitted scarves and mittens. A man arranged jars of honey and jam with handwritten labels. Children ran between the booths, their excitement infectious. It was nothing like the European-style Christmas markets that had become popular in cities. There was no uniformity, no commercial vendors, and no admission fees. Just neighbors sharing food that they'd made.

"Laura." Gabe appeared at her elbow. "Walk with me?"

She nodded and fell into step beside him. They moved slowly around the perimeter, taking in the growing bustle. Neither spoke at first, but she could feel his watchful eye.

"Are you okay with this?" he asked quietly.

"I think so. It's different enough." She paused. "How about you?"

"Ask me in an hour."

They completed their circuit and stopped near a booth where a woman was setting up a display of handmade ornaments—glass painted with delicate designs, wooden stars with burned patterns, and angels twisted from wire and beads.

"Oh, these are lovely," Laura said, genuinely charmed. She picked up a small angel, its wire wings catching the light.

"My grandmother taught me," the woman said. "She always said every tree needs at least one angel to watch over the family."

Laura set it down, something tightening in her throat. She'd had an angel on her childhood tree, one her mother had made. She used to put it on her own Christmas trees until this year. She hadn't put up a tree.

Amid the market preparations, she and Gabe drifted apart. He helped carry boxes but had to stop when his scarred hand wouldn't cooperate. So he chatted with vendors while Laura wandered. The market opened for business, and more people arrived. Soon, the market was bustling while the sound system played classic carols.

Laura found herself pressed between families with strollers, groups of friends laughing loudly, and people stopping abruptly to take photos. The noise level had risen gradually—overlapping conversations, vendor calls, and children's excited shrieks, all mixed with the Christmas music from multiple speakers.

She didn't notice when her breathing changed, but Gabe did.

"Hey." Gabe's hand touched her elbow, gentle but grounding. "You okay?"

She started to nod automatically, then paused. Her chest felt tight. The crowd seemed to pulse around them—too many bodies, too much movement. A child ran past, bumping her hip, and she flinched hard.

The Winter Village memories returned. How quickly the crowd had turned from festive to panicked. How the press of bodies had become dangerous, with everyone trying to run, but they had nowhere to go.

"Laura." Gabe's voice cut through the rising static in her head. He'd moved closer, his body creating a buffer between her and the worst of the crowd. "Let's get some air."

He didn't wait for her to answer but simply guided her with a light touch on her back, navigating through the crowd with surprising efficiency. He seemed to know exactly where the gaps would be, when to pause, and when to move. Within moments, they were at the edge of the market where it opened onto a quieter section of the square.

There was a bench beneath a snow-laden pine, set back from the main thoroughfare. He led her there, and she sank onto it gratefully. The noise was muted here, the crowd a distant river rather than an ocean threatening to drown her.

"Better?" He sat beside her, not too close but close enough that she could feel his solid presence.

"How did you know?" Her voice came out steadier than she expected.

"Your shoulders went up. Your eyes started darting around, looking for exits." He paused. "I do the same thing. When it gets too much."

She looked at him then, seeing the tension in his jaw and the way his own breathing was deliberately controlled.

"You feel it too. The crowds."

"Every time." He was watching the market, but she could tell he was tracking movement, noting positions, and maintaining awareness even while sitting still. "But I've learned to manage it. Mostly."

"By knowing where the exits are?"

"By knowing I'm not trapped." He turned to her. "That's what gets me—feeling trapped. The crowd at Bryant Park—when the shots started, everyone was trying to run, but there was nowhere to go..."

He trailed off, and she found herself reaching over to touch his hand where it rested on his knee. He turned his palm up, letting their fingers interlace.

"It's easier with someone who gets it," she said softly.

"Yeah." His thumb brushed across hers, a simple gesture that somehow steadied them both. "We don't have to pretend it's fine when it's not."

He brought her a coffee, and the warm drink helped ground her. For several minutes, they sat, hands linked, watching the market from their safe distance. The panic that had been building within her dissolved gradually, replaced by a comforting sense of not being alone.

"Thank you," she said. "For noticing. For getting me out."

"We look out for each other," he said simply. "That's what we do now."

The way he said it, with a matter-of-fact certainty, gripped her with an emotion that caught in her throat.

"Ready to go back?" he asked. "We can stick to the edges and avoid the thick of it."

She squeezed his hand. "I'd like that."

They kept to the outskirts of the market, and as they walked, Gabe kept her hand in his in a way that made

Laura feel protected and connected, two people who understood each other's ghosts.

Gabe walked on her left, keeping himself between her and the densest part of the crowd. She wasn't sure if he was doing it consciously, but she was grateful either way.

Then, at a table of used books, she found a worn copy of poetry that she tucked under her arm. Gradually, the anxiety faded to something manageable.

They were passing the ornament booth again when Laura stopped. The wire angel was still there, catching the afternoon sun.

"Wait here," Gabe said quietly.

She watched him approach the vendor and saw them exchange a few words. Money changed hands. He returned with something small wrapped in tissue paper.

"You looked at it earlier," he said, offering her the package. "Before everything happened."

Laura unwrapped it. The angel was even prettier up close, with wire wings that were delicate yet strong and a beaded body that caught the light. Something about its simple beauty, and the fact that he had noticed her looking at it before her panic attack, moved her deeply.

"Thank you," she whispered.

"'Every tree needs an angel,'" he quoted. "Next year's tree, maybe."

She looked up at him, surprised by the gentleness in his voice. His expression was soft, understanding, and caring in a way that made her pulse skip.

"I don't have anything for you," she said.

"You stayed," he said simply. "When I was bleeding out at that market, you stayed. That's worth more than any gift."

They were standing close now, closer than necessary. Laura could see the flecks of gold in his eyes and could smell the wool of his coat mixed with something clean and masculine. For a moment, the surrounding market faded to background noise.

Then a child ran between them, chasing a runaway balloon, and the spell broke. But instead of awkwardness, Laura found herself laughing—a surprisingly genuine sound she hadn't made in months.

Gabe's mouth curved into a smile. "What?"

"Nothing. Just... here we are, after everything, standing in a Christmas market."

"It's progress," he agreed, and then his smile faded as he gazed at her softly.

They resumed their circuit, but something had changed. The distance they'd maintained was gone, replaced by something easier. Their arms brushed as they walked.

Near the end of the market, they found a cart with roasted chestnuts and smoke rising into the cold air. The man tending it looked like he'd stepped out of a Dickens novel, with a full white beard, round cheeks red from the cold, and fingerless gloves.

"Roasted chestnuts!" he called out, though barely anyone was buying.

"Two bags?" the man asked with a knowing smile.

"Just one," Gabe said. "We'll share."

They found a spot at the edge of the square where they could watch the market without being in it. The chestnuts felt warm through the paper bag, and they took turns pulling them out, burning their fingers slightly, laughing at their attempts to peel them while wearing gloves.

"My grandmother used to make these," Laura said. "Every Christmas Eve. The whole house would smell like them."

"Mine too. Though mine usually burned half of them."

"But you ate them anyway."

"Of course. You can't tell a grandmother her chestnuts are burned."

Laura laughed again, easier this time. "The burned ones were part of the tradition."

"Exactly."

They sat for a while, sharing chestnuts and stories, until the sun went behind a cloud, putting a chill in the air.

Gabe said, "What do you say we go inside and warm up by the fire?"

"That sounds amazing."

As they headed back to the inn, the market appeared to be winding down. As they passed Yolanda, who was packing up her remaining goods, Gabe said, "Closing down already?"

The woman said, "Oh, yes. We've got a busy day ahead with the church service and Christmas dinner."

"Oh." Laura wondered if anything would be open for dinner, but before she could ask, the woman said,

"Of course you'll come! Everyone does. It's after church in the fellowship hall."

She and Gabe exchanged looks, and he shrugged as if to say, "Why not?"

Laura smiled at the woman. "I guess we'll see you there, then."

As they continued on their way to the inn, she looked down at their joined hands and thought about how strange this was. Five days ago, she'd boarded a train alone, planning to spend Christmas in solitude. Now she was holding hands with a stranger who wasn't really a stranger, in a town that shouldn't exist, feeling more connected than she had in years.

As they reached the inn's entrance, Laura realized something that stopped her in her tracks. She'd spent an entire afternoon at a Christmas market—surrounded by carols and crowds and holiday chaos—and she'd survived it. More than survived. She'd found moments of actual joy.

"What is it?" Gabe asked, concerned by her sudden stillness.

"I'm okay," she said, wondering at the truth of it. "For the first time in a year, I think I'm actually okay."

He squeezed her hand gently. "Good."

Laura touched the angel in her pocket. It was such a simple thing, but it felt like a promise that, even after the worst year, two broken people could find hope together.

CHAPTER SEVEN

Inside the inn, Mrs. Wright had set up hot cocoa and cookies in the parlor. They collapsed into chairs by the fire—not the same chairs as last night, Laura noticed, but closer together, the distance between them shrinking by degrees.

After browsing the books on the shelf, they each chose a book and settled down to read in companionable silence. But the comfortable chair and the warmth of the fire lulled Laura to a light sleep. She awoke with a start to the hourly church bells, then she saw Gabe's gentle gaze and relaxed.

"I should clean up before church," Laura said, though she made no move to rise.

"Me too," Gabe agreed, equally stationary.

They sat there instead, watching the fire with a new sense of shared peace. She said, "I feel like I've found something I'd lost."

He waited with a curious but patient expression.

She added, "Myself, I guess." The realization

brought emotions she had to tamp down. "I knew who I was before the market. A teacher. Someone who believed in kindness and safety and the basic goodness of people. But..." She trailed off, then started again. "I lost that. I became someone who jumps at loud noises and can't listen to Christmas carols."

"You're someone who stays," Gabe said quietly. "When everyone else runs, you stay. That's who you are to me."

The words settled over her with the warmth of a blanket. She wanted to argue, to point out that staying beside him at the market had been paralysis, not courage. But looking at his face, at the certainty in his eyes, she found that she couldn't.

"Maybe I'm finding that person again. What about you?" she asked instead. "Who are you now that you're not a cop?"

He was quiet for a long moment. "I'm still figuring that out. For seventeen years, the badge was everything. It gave me purpose, structure, and a reason to get up in the morning. Without it..." He flexed his damaged hand unconsciously. "Being here seems to help in a strange sort of way."

"Do you have people back home?" Laura asked. "Friends who... who get it?"

"A few. My friend Tom and his wife, Monica, have tried to be supportive. Although they keep inviting me to dinner, trying to set me up—first with Monica's yoga instructor, then a friend from her book club... Well, you get the idea. With any luck, she'll run out of friends." He laughed. "They mean well."

A clock chimed somewhere in the inn, and Laura realized with surprise that it was already after four. The church service was at six, and then the dinner would follow. She desperately needed a hot shower and clean clothes.

"I should go," she said, finally standing with a groan as her muscles protested.

"Laura." His voice stopped her at the doorway. "Will you go with me?"

"Yes," she said before he could finish. "I'd love that."

She climbed the stairs to her room and found herself thinking about the day. It wasn't the Christmas she had planned, alone in an empty beach town, enjoying a book and her solitude. But as she dried her hair and put on her one nice dress—a deep blue wool she'd packed on impulse—she realized she wasn't sorry. Whatever had brought her to this impossible town, whatever magic was at work here, had given her something she hadn't even known she was missing: connection.

She could hear other guests moving through the hallways, preparing for dinner. Families calling to each other, doors opening and closing, the sounds of community that had been absent from her life for so long. And somewhere in this inn, Gabe was probably standing at his own mirror, preparing to face a crowd because they had promised to go together.

The thought of going together didn't scare her as much as it might have back home. Maybe it was the small, friendly nature of this town that had lowered her defenses, or maybe it was the simple fact of being with

Gabe and knowing that he understood. He'd become more than just the wounded cop from the market. He was someone real to her—a man with dry humor and strong, steady arms and a way of making her feel less alone.

Laura looked at herself in the mirror one last time. Her cheeks were flushed. She blamed the warm shower. But her eyes looked brighter than they had in months. She looked alive, she realized with some surprise. For the first time in a year, she looked like someone who was living rather than just surviving.

She made her way back downstairs, where Gabe was already waiting in the lobby. He had changed into dark jeans and a burgundy sweater that brought out warm tones in his skin. He looked absolutely handsome. When he saw her, his expression shifted into something soft and appreciative.

"You look beautiful," he said simply.

"Thank you." She felt heat rise to her cheeks. "You clean up pretty well yourself."

He offered her his arm, a gesture that ordinarily might have felt unexpected or awkward but instead felt perfectly natural. She took it, and they walked out into the winter evening together.

The church stood at the far end of the square, its stone walls rising in Gothic splendor against the night sky. This was no simple country church but a grand stone relic from the town's 1890s heyday. Its spire reached toward the stars, and its arched windows glowed with stained glass. Snow dusted the carved stonework and gathered in the angles of flying buttresses. As they approached, Laura could hear the deep resonance of the organ warming up with sounds that seemed to vibrate through the very stones.

"We don't have to go in," Gabe said quietly, sensing her hesitation.

"No, I want to. It's just…" She took a breath. "I haven't been to church since my grandmother died, and not at all since the market."

"We can leave whenever you want."

She squeezed his arm gently in thanks, and they climbed the wide stone steps together. Inside, the cathedral took her breath away with soaring vaulted ceilings that disappeared into shadow above, massive stone pillars marching down the nave, and hundreds of white candles flickering in iron sconces along the walls. The air was cool despite the crowd, that particular stone church coolness that never quite warms, and it smelled of evergreen.

Mrs. Wright waved them over to a pew near the middle where she'd saved seats. "I hoped you'd come," she said warmly. "The men and boys choir here is extraordinary."

They settled into the worn wooden pew, and Laura was acutely aware of Gabe beside her, their shoulders almost touching in the narrow space. Around them, the congregation filled every available seat—families in their Sunday best clothes, elderly couples who'd likely sat in the same pews for decades, and young parents trying to quiet restless toddlers.

The organ fell silent. Then, from the back of the cathedral, she heard them—the pure, clear voices of the choir beginning to process. The congregation rose as one, and Laura stood with them, turning to watch.

They came down the center aisle in two lines, men and boys in traditional robes of deep red with white surplices, their voices already raised in the processional hymn. The youngest boys led, some no more than eight or nine, their faces serene and focused. Behind them came the older boys and then the men, their deeper voices providing the foundation for the crystalline soprano of the children.

They took their places in the choir stalls that flanked the altar, the carved wooden seats that had held centuries of singers before them. The conductor, a distinguished man with silver hair, took his place, and the congregation sat.

The cathedral fell into profound silence.

Then, from the front row of the choir, a single boy's voice rose. He couldn't have been more than ten, with dark hair neatly combed and the face of a Renaissance cherub. He simply opened his mouth, and the first notes of "Once in Royal David's City" floated out.

The purity of his voice in that stone space was almost unbearable in its beauty. Each note seemed to hang in the air, the acoustics of the cathedral lifting and carrying the sound until it felt like the very walls were singing. There was no hesitation in his voice, no nervousness—just the absolute clarity of a child who had been trained to perfection but had not yet learned to be self-conscious about the gift he carried.

Laura felt tears slide down her cheeks, and she didn't even think to wipe them away. This wasn't the kind of crying that came from sadness or even from joy —it was simply the body's response to encountering something so beautiful that it overwhelmed every defense. The boy's voice was like light itself, pure and clear, untouched by the darkness she'd carried for a year.

When the last note of the choir faded into the rafters, the silence that followed was full of a sense of the sacred that lingered in the air. Laura became aware of Gabe's shoulder pressed against hers, solid and warm. Around them, others were stirred back to life. Soft murmurs of appreciation rippled through the space. Laura finally raised her hand to wipe her face dry and caught Gabe gazing at her. Their eyes met for just a moment, and an understanding passed between them. They had both been somewhere else for those few minutes, lifted by grace they hadn't known they were seeking.

The service ended, and as people began to move on to their evening plans, Laura and Gabe remained still a heartbeat longer before the moment fully dissolved. Something between them had changed in that hushed, holy space.

CHAPTER EIGHT

—————

Laura woke earlier than usual and took in the stillness of the inn before the new day. Through the window, the world looked crystallized by the layer of frost that glittered like diamonds in the early light. The storm had passed in the night, leaving behind a sky so clear and blue it hurt to look at it.

She dressed in layers, knowing the day would be cold despite the sun. In the hallway, she paused outside Gabe's door, listening for signs of movement. Nothing. She continued downstairs, where Mrs. Wright was already bustling around the dining room, setting out breakfast.

"You're up early, dear," the innkeeper said.

"I've got a train to catch," Laura said brightly.

As soon as she said it, Mrs. Wright's expression fell. "They've cleared the tracks, but the signals are out. I'm afraid you're here for one more day." She smiled and filled Laura's cup. "But the coffee's fresh, and you've got time for a full breakfast."

Laura thanked her and realized she wasn't too disappointed to spend one more day here. In so many ways, her stay here had been better than anything she had planned for herself. She settled back in her seat by the window and watched the town wake up. A few early risers were already out, their breath clouding in the frigid air. The scrape of metal on concrete as someone shoveled their walk carried in the early morning stillness.

"Couldn't sleep?"

She turned to find Gabe behind her, hair still damp from a shower, wearing a thick fisherman's sweater that made him look younger somehow and less guarded.

She gestured toward the chair opposite her. "Just thinking," she said.

He joined her, and after Mrs. Wright brought him coffee, they sat and gazed out the window. It was becoming easy to be with him. The careful distance of their first day had dissolved into something that felt more than comfortable. It felt right.

"I heard some of the locals talking yesterday," he said after a while. "There's a pond about a half-mile behind the town. Apparently, it freezes solid enough for skating."

"That sounds nice," Laura said neutrally.

"Want to go see it? After breakfast?"

She hesitated. "You mean... to skate?"

He smiled. "Well, yes. I thought it might be fun."

Inwardly relieved, Laura said, "Sadly, I haven't got any skates."

"Not a problem. Mrs. Wright has a collection of spares that she loans out to guests."

Laura winced. *Of course she does*. "I should probably tell you—I don't actually know how to skate."

He looked surprised. "Really? I figured growing up in New York..."

"My parents weren't the skating type. They were more the 'museums and libraries' type." She smiled ruefully. "I tried once in college, but I spent more time on my backside than on my feet."

"I could teach you," he offered, then seemed to catch himself.

She'd already guessed the answer but asked, anyway. "Because you really know how to skate?"

He smirked as though it were nothing. "I played hockey in college."

Laura was already imagining herself on the ice. It was not a pretty picture.

Gabe said, "I mean, it's just an idea to pass the time. If you want. No pressure."

Laura considered. The thought of being that unsteady, that vulnerable, made her nervous. But there was something in his expression—hopeful, almost eager —that made her want to try.

"Okay," she said. "But when I fall and take you down with me, remember this was your idea."

His smile transformed his face. "Deal."

After a breakfast of Mrs. Wright's French toast with real maple syrup, they bundled up in their warmest clothes. Mrs. Wright directed them to the pond, insisting they take a thermos of hot chocolate "for after, when you'll need warming up."

The path wound through a small wood behind the town, where the trees were heavy with snow. Their footsteps crunched in the quiet, while the only other sound was an occasional crack of a branch releasing its burden of snow. The cold was sharp enough to make Laura sniffle, but the air felt clean in her lungs.

"So I guess you must have skated a lot as a kid," she said.

"Every winter. There was a rink at our community rec center. My dad would take my sister and me." His voice carried a warmth she hadn't heard before. "He'd been a decent hockey player in high school, so he taught me, and I loved it. They used to stop me all the time for speeding too fast around the outside of the rink. But someone spotted me and recruited me for a local youth team."

"Your sister skated too?"

"Better than me, though I'd never admit it to her face." He ducked under a low branch, holding it up for Laura to pass. "She went the figure skating route and competed a little through high school. She was so graceful on the ice. She made it look effortless."

"Do you still see her?"

"Not as much as I should." A shadow crossed his face. "After the shooting, I kind of... withdrew from everyone. She tried to help, but we live too far apart, and I wasn't ready to be helped."

Laura understood that. She'd done the same with her friends and her colleagues. It was easier to be alone with trauma than to try to explain it to people who couldn't possibly understand.

The trees opened suddenly, and there it was—a perfect oval of ice surrounded by snow-covered banks. The pond was larger than Laura had expected, about the size of a baseball diamond.

Several couples were already on the ice, along with a group of teenagers showing off and an elderly man in the middle doing perfect figure eights with an ease that spoke of decades of practice. On the far bank, someone had built a fire in a metal drum, with logs arranged around it as makeshift benches.

"It's beautiful," Laura breathed.

"Yeah," Gabe agreed, but when she glanced at him, he was looking at her, not the pond. He caught himself and looked away.

On the near end of the pond was a warming hut, a small wooden structure that looked like it had been there forever. Laura sat on a bench to lace up, her gloved hands already clumsy with cold. Gabe knelt in front of her without asking, taking over the lacing.

"They need to be tighter than you think," he said, pulling the laces taut. "It's all about ankle support."

She watched his bent head, the concentration on his face as he worked. He managed surprisingly well with his damaged hand, which seemed steadier today. When he finished with her skates, he looked up, and their faces were suddenly very close.

"Thank you," she said softly.

"You haven't fallen yet," he replied with a mischievous grin. "Save the thanks for after."

He stood and offered her his hands. "Ready?"

"No," she said honestly, but she took his hands, anyway.

The moment her blades hit the ice, Laura knew she was in trouble. Her ankles wanted to bend inward, her knees locked, and her center of gravity seemed to have relocated to somewhere ahead of her skates. Only Gabe's grip kept her upright.

"Okay, first thing—bend your knees," he instructed. "I know it feels wrong, but trust me."

She tried, but her body rebelled against the instability. "I'm going to fall."

"No, you're not. I've got you." His hands were firm on hers, steady and sure. "Bend your knees, lean forward slightly—not too far. Your body wants to be slightly over your feet, not behind them."

She adjusted incrementally, finding a position that felt marginally less precarious.

"Good. Now, don't try to walk. Push sideways with one foot, glide on the other."

"That makes no sense."

"Watch." He let go of one of her hands, demonstrating the motion while still supporting her. The grace of his movement, even while holding her up, made it look effortless.

Laura tried to imitate him and immediately started to fall backward. Gabe's arm came around her waist, pulling her against him to steady her. She grabbed his shoulder instinctively, and suddenly they were pressed together, her face against his shoulder.

"I've got you," he said quietly, his breath warm against her ear.

She nodded, not trusting her voice. This close, she could smell a faint hint of shampoo and feel the solid strength of him through their layers of clothing. Her heart was racing, but not from fear of falling.

"Let's try again," he said, but didn't immediately let go. Keeping one arm around her waist, he said, "Push with your outside foot," he instructed. "I'll match your pace."

They moved slowly, with Laura making tiny pushes while Gabe essentially held her up. But after a few minutes, she started to feel the rhythm of it—push, glide, push, glide.

"You're getting it," he encouraged.

"I'm basically using you as a crutch."

"That's what I'm here for."

They made it halfway around the pond before Laura's confidence got ahead of her skill. She pushed too hard, her free foot slid wide, and suddenly she was going down. Gabe tried to catch her, but her flailing threw him off balance. They landed in a tangle of limbs, Gabe taking the brunt of the impact, with Laura landing mostly on top of him.

For a moment, they just lay there, stunned. Then Laura started laughing—helpless laughter that shook her whole body.

"I warned you," she gasped between giggles. "I said I'd take you down with me."

He was laughing too, his chest vibrating under her. "It's worth it."

She became aware that she was essentially lying on top of him, their faces very close. His laughter faded, and his eyes darkened as he looked at her. The world seemed to narrow until there were only the two of them on the ice, the warmth of his body contrasting with the cold beneath them as his hand came up to rest on her back.

"Laura," he said softly.

A spray of ice chips hit them as one of the teenagers hockey stopped nearby. "You folks okay?" the kid asked, grinning.

The spell broke. Gabe helped Laura sit up, then stand, both of them brushing snow from their clothes.

"We're fine," Gabe told the teenager as he rubbed his scarred hand. "Just practicing."

"Maybe try staying vertical," the kid suggested cheerfully before skating off.

"Punk," Gabe muttered, but he was smiling.

They tried again, and this time Laura lasted longer before her next fall. Gabe caught her properly this time, spinning her into his arms rather than letting her hit the ice. For a moment, they stood frozen, her hands on his chest, his arms around her waist.

"You're improving," he said.

"I have a good teacher."

Laura realized they were standing too close and gazing too long, but she couldn't help herself. Around them, other skaters glided by. Couples held hands, the elderly man glided along with one leg extended behind him, and the teenagers wove in and out of people as they played tag. But here with Gabe, Laura felt separate from it all, as if she and Gabe existed in their own bubble of space and time.

"Again?" he asked.

"Again."

This time, he said, "I'm going to let go for just a second. You can do this."

"Don't you dare—"

But he'd already released her, although she could feel him close by, ready to catch her. She wobbled, windmilled her arms, but stayed upright. She was skating. Slowly and barely, but actually skating on her own.

"I'm doing it!" she exclaimed, then immediately lost her balance.

Gabe caught her around the waist and pulled her against him. "You were," he agreed, sounding amused.

"For three seconds," she said, wincing.

"It counts," he insisted.

"Yeah, it does count, doesn't it?"

They continued around the pond, with Gabe gradually giving her more independence but never moving far from catching distance. She fell several more times, but less dramatically each time as she learned how to catch herself or at least control the descent.

Other skaters offered encouragement as they passed. An older couple, moving in perfect synchronization after what looked like decades together, smiled warmly at them. The woman called out, "You're doing great!"

"They think we're together," Laura said quietly to Gabe.

"Aren't we?" he asked, then seemed to catch

himself. "I mean, we're literally together here—on the ice."

"Right."

They made it three full circuits of the pond before Laura's ankles began to protest. "I think I need a break," she admitted.

They made their way to the fire, where several others had gathered to warm up. Someone had brought marshmallows and was passing them around to roast on sticks. Gabe found them a log to sit on, and Laura gratefully sank, her legs shaking from the unfamiliar exertion.

"Hot chocolate?" Gabe suggested, producing Mrs. Wright's thermos.

The chocolate was still warm, rich, and dark with dissolving whipped cream. They passed the cup back and forth, watching the skaters circle the pond. In the midday sun, the ice gleamed like polished silver.

"Thank you," Laura said. "For being a patient teacher."

"You're a quick learner."

She laughed. "Yeah, a dozen falls later."

"But you got back up each time." He turned to her with a serious look. "That's what matters."

She suspected they weren't merely talking about skating anymore. Over the past few days, they'd been through her panic attacks, the discovery of their shared trauma, and the slow building of trust.

He was quiet for a moment, watching the fire. "I haven't managed to get up and move on from the shooting. It wasn't so much what happened at the market. It was after—being forced to retire. A cop was all I knew how to be."

"So, what now?"

"Now I'm beginning to realize there might be more to me—or to life—than the badge." He glanced at her. "These last few days have been... different. In a good way."

The thought filled her with warmth. "For me too."

They sat quietly for a while, finishing the hot chocolate and watching the other skaters. The elderly man was teaching one of the teenagers how to skate backward. The synchronized couple had left, replaced by a young family with a small child taking his first tentative slides between his parents.

"Want to try again?" Gabe asked. "Or have you had enough for one day?"

Laura considered. Her ankles hurt, her tailbone was definitely bruised, and she'd probably be sore tomorrow. But there was something about being out there with him, his hands steady on her waist, and the shared laughter when she inevitably fell.

"Once more around?" she suggested.

His smile was answer enough.

This time, she made it halfway around the pond before falling, and when Gabe caught her, spinning her into his arms to prevent the fall, she stayed. With her hands on his shoulders and his arms around her waist, their smiles faded, and they looked into each other's eyes.

"Laura," he started.

"I know," she said softly.

He leaned down, closing the distance between them. She could feel his breath warm on her face as his lips were an inch from hers. Her lips parted.

A child's shriek of laughter broke the moment as the family's toddler took a spectacular tumble nearby. Both parents rushed to help, the child more delighted than hurt, and Laura and Gabe moved apart.

"We should probably head back," Laura said, her voice not quite steady.

"Yeah," Gabe agreed, but he took her hand as they skated slowly toward the bank.

They wordlessly unlaced their skates and walked back through the woods slowly, in no hurry for the afternoon to end. As they walked along, the sun was beginning to slant through the trees. Their hands brushed together, and Gabe took hers and laced their fingers together.

"I can't remember the last time I did anything like that," Laura said. "Just had fun without thinking about anything else."

"When did we stop doing that?" Gabe wondered. "Being able to laugh at ourselves when we fall."

Laura said, "When the world taught us that sometimes it's too hard to get up."

He squeezed her hand. "But we did. And we're here."

"We are," she said, and then added what she'd been thinking all afternoon. "I'm glad I met you. It's helped me to look at things differently—to think about moving forward."

"You would have," he said with certainty. "You're stronger than you know. But I feel the same way, too."

They emerged from the woods to find the town bathed in late afternoon light. The square was quieter than yesterday, with most people inside preparing for the evening. Through windows, Laura could see families gathering, lights being lit, the ordinary magic of daily life continuing.

They stood on the inn's porch, still holding hands, neither quite ready to go inside and end this moment. The angel in Laura's pocket pressed gently against her hip, a reminder of yesterday's small triumph.

"Thank you," she said again. "For today. For the skating lesson. For catching me all those times."

"Always," he said simply, and something in his voice made it sound like a vow.

They stamped snow from their boots in the vestibule, fingers still tingling from the cold despite their gloves. Laura was laughing about her last spectacular fall when they pushed through into the lobby.

Mrs. Wright looked up from the front desk, and something in her expression made them both stop. Not disapproval exactly—more like a cautious parent watching children dance around something obvious.

As she collected their borrowed skates, she said, "You two look frozen through," she said warmly. "I've kept the fire going in the parlor. Tea?"

"That would be wonderful," Laura said, already moving toward the warmth.

They settled into the wingback chairs, closer together than they'd sat before. Mrs. Wright arrived with a full tray, complete with teapot, cups, cream, sugar, and a plate of shortbreads.

"Mrs. Wright," Gabe said as she poured, "can I ask you something?"

"Of course, dear."

"How long has Evergreen Junction been here?"

Her hands didn't pause, but her smile changed—became something older, wiser. "Oh, a very long time. Although not everyone sees it."

Laura and Gabe exchanged glances.

"I don't understand," Laura said carefully.

Mrs. Wright settled into a chair across from them, seeming to prepare words she'd been waiting to say. "The town has always been here for many decades, but the train..." She gestured vaguely toward the depot. "This isn't a regular stop. On most nights, it passes right by us. I'm told people look out their train windows and see nothing but forest."

"But on Christmas Eve we stopped," Gabe prompted.

"Christmas Eve is special." Her eyes held that knowing quality again. "On Christmas Eve, the train stops for people who..." She chose her words carefully, "...need to find something they've lost—or someone. Sometimes it's both."

The fire crackled. Outside, snow continued to fall.

"How long does it stay here?" Laura asked, though something told her she already knew the answer.

"Until the gifts have been given." Mrs. Wright stood, smoothing her skirt. "Sometimes that takes a while. In my experience, the most important gifts are the ones we're most afraid to give."

She rose and moved toward the door, then paused. "I've heard that the morning train leaves at 10:45. The signal repairs should be complete by then." She turned to leave but turned back. "Some people, once they leave Evergreen Junction, try to find their way back. But that rarely happens."

She left them alone with the fire, the tea, and their thoughts.

CHAPTER NINE

THE TAVERN WAS warm and inviting, with a fire crackling softly in the corner. Gabe and Laura had claimed a small table near the window, where they could watch the snow fall outside while they enjoyed burgers and fries.

Around them, other patrons spoke in low voices with the easy familiarity of people who'd known each other for years. A couple played darts in the corner. Two old men at the bar argued good-naturedly about something. The atmosphere was inviting yet intimate.

"More water?" the bartender asked, already reaching for Laura's empty glass.

"Please," she said.

Gabe's glass was still half full, sitting just out of his reach. Without thinking, he reached for it with his left hand—the damaged one—intending to slide it closer so the bartender could refill both at once.

His fingers closed around the glass. Then spasmed.

The glass slipped, hit the edge of the table, and

exploded on the wooden floor with a sound like a gunshot.

The entire room went silent.

Every head turned. Conversations stopped mid-word. The dart players froze. Even the jukebox in the corner seemed to fade.

In that silence, the sound of glass shards skittering across the floor was deafening.

"I'm so sorry," Gabe said, his voice tight.

"No problem at all!" The bartender was already there with a broom. "Happens all the time."

But it didn't happen all the time. Anyone else would have moved that glass just fine. Anyone else's hand would have worked.

"Gabe—" Laura reached for his arm.

"Don't." He pulled away, standing abruptly. "I need some air."

He was already moving toward the door before she could respond. Laura threw cash on the table and followed him outside.

The cold hit immediately. He stood in the middle of the snowy street with his back to her, his hands shoved deep in his pockets, and his shoulders were rigid with tension.

"It's just a glass," she said quietly.

"It's not just a glass." His tone was hard and defensive. "It's everything. Every stupid thing I try to do. I can't hold a weapon. I can't do my job. I can't even—" He broke off.

She moved closer. "It's still healing."

"No, it's not." He spun to face her, and the bitter

look in his eyes made her stop. "This is it, Laura. This is as good as it gets. The surgeons told me. The nerves are too damaged. I'll never get full function back."

"I know that. But—"

"Do you?" He pulled his left hand from his pocket, held it up in the lamplight. The tremor was visible even from where she stood. "I'm broken. Permanently. And I keep pretending I'm not, keep acting like eventually I'll be fine, but I won't be. This is who I am now."

"So what?" The words came out sharper than she intended. "You think that matters to me?"

"It should." He let his hand drop. "You should be with someone who's got their crap together. Not someone who can't hold a frigging glass of water without dropping it."

The words hit her like a slap. "Is that what you think? That I need someone 'together'?" She laughed, but it was bitter. "Look at me, Gabe. I had a panic attack over Christmas decorations. I can't go to Bryant Park without shaking. I avoid crowds and loud noises, and most of the time I feel like I'm just barely holding it together—"

"That's different."

"How is it different?"

"Because you're trying! You came to that market even though you were terrified. You got on that ice even though you'd never skated before. You're brave, Laura. You're—"

"I'm what?"

"Not broken."

She was angry. "Don't do that. Don't put me on

some pedestal while you wallow in—" She stopped. The look on his face made the words die in her throat.

"I'm sorry," she said quietly. "I didn't mean—"

"You're right." His voice was flat now, empty. "I am wallowing in self-pity. And you don't need to be dragged down by that."

"That's not what I said."

"But it's what you meant." He looked away, toward the lights of the inn. "We should get back. It's late."

"Gabe—"

"Please. I just... I need to be alone right now."

He started walking toward the inn. After a moment, she followed, but the distance between them felt like miles.

They climbed the stairs in silence. At her door, she turned to him, wanting to fix this, to take back the words that had come out wrong.

But he was already moving toward his own room, his damaged hand still hidden in his pocket.

"Goodnight, Laura," he said without looking back.

She stood there for a long moment, key in her hand, feeling something breaking between them. Not catastrophically. Just... cracking. Small fissures that would widen if they didn't do something.

"I can't help him," she thought. "I can't even help myself. We're just two broken people."

She went into her room and closed the door.

❄

LAURA SAT on the edge of her bed and replayed the argument. The look on his face when she'd snapped at him. The way he'd pulled away. The cruel accuracy of her words—wallowing—when what she'd meant was something else entirely.

She'd meant to say that she understood, because she did the same thing. Instead, her words came out as judgment, and now the space between their rooms felt like an ocean.

The clock on the nightstand read 11:47. She should change, wash her face, and try to sleep. Tomorrow, they would board the train and go back to their separate lives. This week would become a memory—beautiful and painful and, sadly, unfinished.

GABE STOOD in the hallway outside his room, key in hand, and couldn't make himself go inside.

The look on Laura's face when she'd said *wallowing* kept replaying in his mind. Not anger—he could have handled anger. It was the flash of regret the moment the word left her mouth, the way her expression crumpled when she realized what she'd said.

She'd been right, though. That was the worst part. He had been wallowing, hiding behind his injury like it was a shield against trying, against failing, against wanting things he didn't think he deserved anymore.

He unlocked his door and stepped inside. The room was identical to hers—same quilt, same radiator clanking softly, same view of the snow-covered square.

But it felt hollow without her presence, without the sound of her voice or the way she tucked her hair behind her ear when she was thinking.

Tomorrow morning, they'd board that train. They'd sit in separate cars or pretend to read separate books, and when they reached New York, they'd say a polite goodbye. She'd disappear into the city, and he'd go back to his empty apartment, and that would be the end of it.

He sat on the edge of the bed, his damaged hand resting on his thigh. The tremor was worse now—it always was when he was stressed. She'd seen him at his worst tonight, seen the anger and the self-pity and all the ugliness he usually kept locked down.

And she'd stayed. Even when he'd pushed her away, even when he'd given her every reason to walk away for good, she'd looked at him with those eyes that saw everything and hadn't flinched.

You're brave, he'd told her earlier. He used to be brave. Not anymore. Laura had reached out and asked to be part of his life, but he'd been too scared to reach back.

The clock on the nightstand showed 11:52. In eight hours, they'd be gone. In eight hours, he'd lose the only person who'd made him feel whole since the shooting. The only person who understood what it meant to be broken and still found him worth loving.

No.

The word came from somewhere deep, somewhere that had survived seventeen years of police work, a shooting, and a year of grief. He couldn't do this. He couldn't sit in this room and let fear win. Not again. Not with her.

He stood and walked to the door, his heart hammering against his ribs. His hand shook as he reached for the doorknob—and for once, he didn't care. Let it shake. Let her see every damaged part of him. She deserved the truth, and the truth was that he loved her. Broken hand, ruined career, uncertain future—none of it mattered as much as the chance to tell her that.

The hallway was empty and quiet. Three doors down, light showed beneath her door. She was still awake.

He walked toward it before he could think better of it, before the fear could talk him out of it. At her door, he raised his hand and knocked softly. He wouldn't blame her for not opening the door. He deserved to be ignored.

A SOFT KNOCK at her door made her heart jump. She knew it couldn't be anyone else. For a second, she paused with her hand on the doorknob, then opened the door.

"I'm sorry," he said immediately. "For pushing you away. For snapping at you. For—"

"I'm sorry too. I shouldn't have said that about wallowing. I didn't mean it the way it sounded."

"Can I come in?"

She moved back without hesitation. He stepped inside, and she closed the door behind him, enclosing them in the small space. For a moment, they just stood there, looking at each other in the dim light from her bedside lamp.

"I don't know how to do this," he said quietly. "Be here for somebody else when I'm just a broken version of who I used to be."

"You're not broken—"

"I am." He moved closer. "We both are. And I keep thinking that means we shouldn't... that I shouldn't..."

"Shouldn't what?"

He wanted to cup her face in his hands, even despite the damaged one, tremor and all. But he couldn't bring himself to. "I shouldn't want you the way I do, or ask you to take on someone who can't even hold a glass without dropping it."

"I don't care about the glass."

"You should."

"Well, I don't." She lifted her hand and nearly reached out, but then let it drop. "And if we're making confessions, I shouldn't want you either. I shouldn't drag you into my mess—the panic attacks, the fear, all the ways I'm still stuck in that day a year ago."

"Laura—"

"But I do. I want you." The words came out in a rush. "I know it's impossibly complicated and messy and probably a terrible idea—"

Ask her. A voice in his head insisted. *Ask her into your life. Get her number. Her address. Make sure you can find her after tonight. Do not let her go.*

But the words stuck in his throat. If he asked—if he made this real by planning for tomorrow—he'd have to face what he'd become. He couldn't even imagine a future alone, let alone with somebody else. There was a time when he wouldn't have hesitated to sweep Laura into his arms and begin dreaming of a future together. But he wasn't that man anymore. He wasn't the cop who had tackled a shooter. He was merely a man who couldn't hold a glass without dropping it. He was a man whose career was over, whose identity had been stripped away, and who woke every morning to a man in the mirror he didn't recognize.

He had nothing to give her. She deserved someone who was moving forward, not someone still drowning in what he'd lost in the past.

Maybe tomorrow. He tried to convince himself. Maybe I'll be ready tomorrow to ask. When *I've figured out how to be enough for her.* But he knew, even as he thought it, that tomorrow he'd find another reason to wait.

But tomorrow didn't matter. He was here with her now, and he kissed her. He cut off all the doubts and put his mouth, urgent and desperate, on hers. She made a sound of relief or surrender, or both, and wrapped her arms around his neck, pulling him closer.

This kiss was different from the one in the gazebo. That had been wonder and discovery. This kiss was full of desperation and desire—and the knowledge that morning would come too soon. His hands moved from her face to her hair, then down her back, pulling her flush against him. He could feel her heart racing.

When he ended the kiss, he pressed his forehead to hers. "Tell me to leave. Tell me this is a bad idea."

She whispered, "It probably is."

He couldn't argue the point.

"But I don't want it to be." She pulled back just enough to look him in the eyes. "And I want you to stay."

The last of his resistance crumbled. "Are you sure?"

In answer, she kissed him again, slower this time, savoring it.

He found the hem of her sweater, and she lifted her arms to help him pull it over her head. His hands traced the curve of her waist. "You're beautiful," he breathed against her neck.

She reached for the buttons of his shirt with shaking fingers. He helped her, shrugged out of it, and then pulled her close again, skin against skin. The contact was electric, like coming home to a place he'd never been.

They moved toward the bed without breaking apart, a tangle of limbs and whispered words. When he laid her down on the quilt, he paused, looking down at her. The sight made his heart ache.

"We can stop," he said.

"I don't want to."

"Neither do I."

He kissed her again—her mouth, her jaw, the hollow of her throat—and she arched into his touch.

And then there were no more words, just the two of them moving together in the darkness, finding solace in each other's brokenness, and proving that sometimes damaged pieces fit together better than whole ones ever could.

LATER, she lay with her head on his chest, listening to his heartbeat slow down to normal. His arm was wrapped around her, his damaged hand resting on her hip, the tremor barely noticeable now. Through the window, snow continued to fall, covering the world in white.

"I don't want tomorrow to come," she said quietly.

His arm tightened around her. "I know."

"The train leaves at 10:45."

"I know."

The silence stretched between them, heavy with everything they weren't saying. Laura's phone was in her bag, three feet away. She could reach for it right now, hand it to him, and watch him type in his number. Simple.

But then what? Then she'd have to go back to her apartment in the city, back to her panic attacks and all the ways she was still broken. And he'd see it all—not just these three perfect days in a magical town, but the reality of loving someone who fell apart in crowds, who couldn't listen to Christmas carols, and who was still so damaged that getting through each day took so much out of her that there wasn't much left for anyone else.

He deserved better than that, she thought. He deserved someone whole.

Gabe stared at the ceiling, feeling her breathing even out against his chest. He should say something, but what? Apologize for wanting to be with her so much that he let himself, for a moment, believe he could be with her? Normal people did it all the time. They met someone they cared about, fell in love, and built something together. But nothing about this week had been normal.

She had saved his life once. She'd knelt in the snow and pressed her hands against his wound and refused to let him die. What could he give her in return? A broken hand that couldn't hold a glass steady? A ruined career? He might look okay on the outside, but she'd soon discover how damaged he was, and still bleeding from wounds no one could see.

And yet, as he lay here with her in his arms, he couldn't help but believe it was worth it. This feeling—this love—filled his heart. Whether that was enough to leave him content for a lifetime, he couldn't say. But for now, he would savor this night with the woman he loved.

CHAPTER TEN

GABE WOKE to pale gray light filtering through the curtains and the warmth of Laura curved against him. Her hair spread across his chest, one hand resting over his heart. He could feel the gentle rise and fall of her breathing and see the slight flutter of her eyelashes against her cheek.

He didn't move because that would disturb the moment, and then morning would have to arrive. If he stayed still enough, time might not stop, but he could prolong the moment. If only they could exist here forever in this impossible place where the real world couldn't reach them. But his mind was already racing. In the cold light of morning, the complications began to crowd in.

She stirred slightly, pressing closer in her sleep, and his arm tightened around her instinctively. Through the window, he could hear sounds he hadn't noticed before: the steady drip of water, icicles melting in the sun, the soft patter against the windowsill.

He tried to memorize her face: the small scar above her left eyebrow he'd discovered last night, the way her mouth curved slightly even in sleep, the freckles scattered across her nose that were invisible until you were this close.

Her breathing changed. She was waking up.

He watched her surface slowly: the flutter of eyelashes, the slight frown as she oriented herself, and the moment her eyes opened and found his. For one heartbeat, her expression was completely open—soft and happy.

Then awareness crept in, and he watched her remember where they were, what they'd done, and what would come next.

"Hi," she whispered.

"Hi."

They looked at each other. He wanted to say something, but the words got caught in his throat.

The phone on the nightstand rang.

They both flinched. Laura pulled back slightly, and he felt the loss of her warmth immediately. He reached for the phone, his other arm reluctant to release her.

"Hello?"

"Mr. Lawson? This is Mrs. Wright. I have wonderful news. The tracks have been cleared. The train will be running on schedule this morning. Departure at 10:45."

His throat closed. "That's... good. Thank you."

"Breakfast will be ready within the hour." She paused and, when she spoke again, her voice carried an inexplicable melancholy. "You know, the train doesn't always stop here, so we're grateful it brought you to us."

"Yeah," he managed. "Me too."

He hung up slowly. Laura was sitting now, the sheet pulled up to her arms. Her hair was a mess, her hazel eyes still looked sleepy, and she'd never looked more beautiful or more out of reach.

"So," she said. "10:45."

"Yeah."

The word sat between them like a stone. They needed to talk. But neither of them moved, and the silence stretched until it became its own statement.

Laura looked down at her hands. "I should—" She gestured vaguely toward the door. "I need to pack."

Don't go. Stay. We'll figure this out. "Laura?"

She looked up, and he saw something flicker in her eyes. Hope, maybe? No, probably fear. But then it was gone, shuttered behind that controlled facade he recognized because he did the same.

He said, "I'll meet you in the lobby."

"Nine-thirty okay?"

He nodded, unable to push words past the tightness in his chest.

She gathered her clothes from where they'd landed on the floor—her sweater inside out and her jeans in a tangle—and she dressed with her back to him. The intimacy of the night had dissolved in the morning light.

At the door, she paused, turned, and smiled, but it didn't reach her eyes.

"See you in a bit."

Then she was gone.

Gabe lay there for a long moment, staring at the ceiling. The bedding smelled like her cologne. The pillow still held the imprint of her head. And he'd just let her walk out without saying any of the things that mattered.

"Coward," he thought savagely and forced himself up.

LAURA STOOD under the shower until the water ran lukewarm, trying to wash away the ache that had settled in her chest. The practical voice in her head—the one that had gotten her through the past year—was already organizing, planning, and protecting.

It was one night. A beautiful night, but still... She knew little about him except that they'd shared one tragic event and one night. They'd never mentioned the future. He lived somewhere, she lived somewhere else, and neither seemed to want more. That was answer enough.

But her body remembered every place his hands had been. She could still feel the touch of his mouth on her neck, and his weight, and the sound of her name in the dark when he murmured it.

She turned the water to cold, gasping at the shock of it. Better. This was better. Wake up. Reality check. The train was leaving at 10:45, and whatever they'd shared in Evergreen Junction would be left behind.

Except she didn't want it to.

She wanted to go back to his room, crawl into his

bed, and tell him—what? That she was falling in love? That the thought of saying goodbye made her feel like she was being torn in half? That she'd never felt this connected to anyone, and she didn't know how to let it go?

But what if he didn't feel the same? What if last night was just... physical? What if saying those things out loud would make him look at her with pity or, worse, polite regret?

Laura dressed mechanically—jeans, sweater, the same clothes she'd worn yesterday. She packed her bag with precise movements, folding each item carefully, avoiding thought. The wire angel went into her coat pocket, its edges pressing against her palm.

In the mirror, her reflection looked the same as always: neat, contained. No one would know that underneath, everything felt raw and exposed.

You're good at this, she reminded herself—at holding it together and not falling apart. You've had enough practice.

Nine-twenty. She picked up her bag and opened the door.

Gabe was standing in the hallway.

They both froze. He looked like he'd been pacing— or standing outside his door. Or maybe they'd just emerged at the same moment by coincidence. His hair was still damp, and he wore the same sweater from last night. They stood three feet apart like strangers.

"I was just—" he started.

"Me too," she said quickly.

They looked at each other. A door opened somewhere down the hall, and they both turned toward the sound. When they looked back, whatever moment had existed was gone.

"Ready?" he said.

"Yeah."

They walked down together, not touching. At the bottom of the stairs, the businessman from their first night was checking out, complaining loudly about the delay to his schedule. His wife caught Laura's eye and then glanced away in embarrassment.

Mrs. Wright was everywhere at once—settling bills, offering directions, and pressing wrapped pastries into hands "for the journey." She beamed when she saw Laura and Gabe descend together.

"There you are! I've packed you both some provisions. The train can be dreadfully slow about food service." She handed them each a paper bag that smelled of fresh bread and coffee, then leaned in conspiratorially and smiled. "We like to think our town has a little miracle for everyone who stays here. I hope you found yours."

"Thank you," Laura's throat tightened, but she managed a smile. "It's been lovely."

In the dining room, other guests were finishing breakfast, discussing their trips home and their plans for the new year. The elderly couple who'd been there all week were staying another night—"Why rush?" the gentleman said cheerfully. The family with teenagers was heading to Boston. Everyone seemed happy to be moving on, eager to get wherever they were going.

Laura and Gabe sat at a small table by the window.

They drank coffee in silence, both looking out at the town square where patches of cobblestone showed through the snow in sunny spots.

"It's strange," Laura said, needing to break the silence. "How fast it's melting."

"Yeah."

She wanted to scream. Last night, they'd barely needed words—every touch, every breath had communicated everything. Now they were reduced to comments about the weather.

"Gabe—"

"Laura—"

They spoke at the same time, then both stopped. They waited for the other to continue. Neither did.

"You first," he finally said.

But whatever she'd been about to say had evaporated. "I just... thank you. For this week. For—everything. For saving me in that square, for teaching me to skate, and for making me laugh... *And for last night, for making me feel alive again when I'd forgotten what that felt like.* Anyway, thank you."

"Yeah," he said again. She wondered if he was struggling, searching for words, or if he had nothing to say. "You, too."

The businessman's voice carried from the lobby. "Well, we'd better get moving if we want good seats. You know how it is when you get bumped to the next train. There's no telling what's left."

Laura checked her watch. Ten o'clock. They gathered their bags and joined the small group heading toward the train station. The morning was warmer than any day since they'd arrived, and the sun made Laura squint.

The businessman and his wife walked ahead, arguing about whether to drive next time. Behind them, the family's teenagers looked miserably bored. At the end of the group, Laura and Gabe walked side by side, shoulders not quite touching.

Laura kept thinking he would say something, but he was uncomfortably withdrawn, and she couldn't bring herself to speak first.

The depot came into view, and anxiety seized her. They were actually leaving. In less than an hour, they'd be on a train heading back home to their separate lives.

"Say something," she thought desperately. But they were climbing the depot steps with the others, and the moment was gone.

The train was already at the platform, and it was packed. Holiday travelers who'd been delayed by the storm were all trying to get home at once, plus the group from Evergreen Junction.

GABE SAW to it that their return seats were together, then they boarded the train. He and Laura were working their way down the aisle together when a bright voice cut through the chaos.

"Oh my gosh, I think those were the only seats left, and we got them!"

A young woman with highlighted blonde hair was pointing at a four-seat configuration near the middle of the car. Two seats on one side, two on the other, the only empty spots visible. Laura's stomach sank.

"Excuse me, excuse me!" The blonde woman pushed through with a man in tow. "Sorry, coming through!"

They all converged on the seats at once—Laura and Gabe from one direction, and the couple from the other. For one awkward moment, they all stopped and looked at one another.

When the ticket agent had said their two tickets were together, Gabe hadn't thought to ask if they'd be facing another couple. Any hope of a private moment with Laura was gone.

The woman looked from the e-ticket on her phone to the seats. "We're here, so you must be there." After gesturing toward the opposite seats, she tilted her head at an angle that managed to be both coy and performative. "We're Kylie and Carter! We just got engaged Christmas night at the gazebo!"

The gazebo. Gabe felt the memory flash through him—Laura backed against the pillar, his mouth on hers, the desperate want of that kiss. He glanced at her and found her eyes on him with what looked like the same memory reflected back.

"Magic place, right?" Carter continued, oblivious.

"Yeah," Gabe said, his voice rougher than intended. "Congratulations."

"Thanks! Please, sit!" Kylie gestured enthusiastically.

Laura slid into the window seat. Gabe took the one beside her—close and yet not close enough. Across the aisle, Kylie settled next to Carter and pulled out her phone.

"I totally saw you two at the inn! You were by the fire and then walking to breakfast. You look so perfect together! Didn't I say that, babe? How long have you been married?"

"We're not—" Laura started.

"We just met," Gabe said at the same time.

"On the train," Laura added quickly.

Kylie's eyes went impossibly wider. "Oh my gosh, so this wasn't like a romantic getaway? No! You just happened to be there? But you're sitting together now!" She clutched Carter's arm. "This is fate! The universe puts people in each other's paths for a reason!"

The train lurched into motion. Through the window, Gabe watched it all disappear. The depot, the path through the pines, and the town square grew smaller. The gazebo was lost behind trees, and then nothing.

Beside him, Laura had gone very still. Her shoulder pressed against his—just barely, hidden from view.

"Kylie thinks everyone should be in love," Carter said fondly. "She's already planning our wedding even though I just proposed two days ago."

"June!" Kylie announced. "But not basic June. Elevated June. Oh, and I make custom essential oil blends for weddings! That's my whole business—Kylie's Essentials. You should follow me on Instagram! What are your handles?"

"I'm not on social media," Gabe said.

Laura shook her head in agreement.

Kylie's mouth fell open. "What? How do people find you? How do you keep up with anything?" She looked genuinely distressed. "My entire business is Instagram! I have seventeen thousand followers!"

Gabe nodded and reached into his pocket, desperate to look busy with anything else, but the screen was black. Dead battery. He'd forgotten to charge it at the inn because he'd been... distracted.

He glanced at Laura, about to ask if she had a charger, when Kylie leaned across the aisle.

"Oh my gosh, is your phone dead? That's like my actual nightmare. Carter, give him your portable charger—no wait, I used it for my selfie light. Sorry!"

Laura was reaching for her bag. "I have a charger." She pulled out her phone, and her thumb hovered over the contacts icon. She glanced up at him, but Gabe averted his eyes.

The PA system crackled to life: "ATTENTION PASSENGERS, WE'RE EXPERIENCING TECH-NICAL DIFFICULTIES—"

The feedback was so loud that everyone winced and covered their ears. When it finally stopped, Laura's phone was back in her purse, and she held out her charger.

Kylie was talking again, and the moment was gone. "—which is why you need backup chargers."

Carter nodded. "She has this whole system. Triple backup. It's brilliant."

She beamed adoringly at her fiancé. "Carter gets me."

"The thing is," Carter interrupted, leaning forward

with the confidence of someone about to impart wisdom, "When you know, you know. Right? Like when I met Kylie—boom. Done. She's the one."

"We were friends for two years first," Kylie added. "But we almost didn't get together because we were scared of ruining the friendship. Can you imagine? What if we'd passed up our shot at happiness because we were afraid?"

Gabe couldn't breathe. Beside him, Laura's hand moved slightly on her armrest, her pinky finger just barely extended toward his side. An invitation or an accident, he couldn't tell.

"No point waiting around when you find something real," Carter continued. "Life's too short."

Gabe's hand started to move toward Laura's, but Kylie started talking.

"So what do you do?"

She looked at Gabe, but when he hesitated, Laura chimed in, "I'm a teacher."

"Oh my gosh, you're a teacher! What grade?"

"Kindergarten."

Kylie gasped. "Kindergarten? Oh, that must be so much fun!"

"Well, it can be, but it's also w—"

"That's perfect!" Kylie interrupted. "Because when Carter and I have our three kids—"

"Two," Carter corrected.

Kylie's eyebrows drew together as she smiled at Carter. "No, babe, three. Anyway..." She turned back to Laura. "I'll totally need your advice! Do you have a card?"

"Uh... no, I don't have cards," Laura said.

"No Instagram, no business cards—you two are like adorable time travelers!" Kylie giggled. "Carter, remember when we tried to exchange numbers at the conference, but my phone died, and yours was in the hotel, and we had to use that cocktail napkin?"

"Which you later spilled coffee on," Carter added.

"But we found each other anyway! Because it was meant to be." She cast sparkling eyes at Carter.

In unison, they said, "When you know, you know."

"Next stop, Penn Station!"

The announcement hung in the air. Gabe felt Laura pull away slightly.

They gathered their belongings and waited to merge into the aisle. Gabe ended up ahead of Laura and turned back to make sure she was there. Their eyes met and held an unspoken question. *What now?* Then the doors opened, and the crowd swept them out of the train.

"Wait, babe, Starbucks!" Kylie's voice carried over the chaos. "Just two seconds!" Carter's resigned sigh was audible even from several feet away. "You guys go ahead. Our rideshare fell through, so we'll see you at the taxi stand."

Gabe and Laura were caught up in the river of people. Holiday travelers pressed in from all sides, voices echoed off the vaulted ceiling, and luggage wheels clattered across tiles. The departure board flashed, updating constantly.

Laura's chest was beginning to tighten. *Just breathe. You can do this. You've done harder things.*

The announcement system crackled to life—that sharp burst of static that always preceded the garbled blare.

And suddenly she wasn't in Penn Station anymore. She was at the Christmas village. The gunshots. The screaming. The way sound distorted when terror took over, and time seemed to slow down, making it hard to react.

Her breath wouldn't come. The crowds pressed closer. No, they weren't closer, but they felt closer—suffocating and trapping her.

"Laura." Gabe's voice cut through the static in her head. His hand found her elbow, steady and warm. "Look at me."

She couldn't. If she looked at him, he'd see. He'd be reminded how broken she still was, how one loud noise in a crowded station could reduce her to this.

"Laura, please." His hand moved to her face, gentle but firm, turning her toward him. "You're okay. You're safe. I've got you."

His eyes locked onto hers, dark and sure, and slowly —so slowly—the station came back into focus. The crowds were just crowds. The announcement was just an announcement. Her breath hitched once, twice, then finally eased into something like normal.

"I'm sorry," she whispered.

"Don't be."

But she could see it in his face—worry, yes, but also something else. The same look he'd had when he dropped the soup bowl. Like he was cataloging the failures, adding this to the list. We can't even get through a train station without one of us falling apart.

"I'm fine," she said, pulling back slightly. "Really. It just caught me off guard."

The businessman from before pushed past them, talking loudly on his phone. His wife followed, hurrying to keep up.

Gabe's jaw tightened. "Maybe we should find somewhere to sit." As he said it, he knew finding an empty place to sit in the crowd would be impossible.

Laura straightened her shoulders. "No, I'm fine. We can go."

As they headed for the exit, the truth settled over Laura. This wasn't just an isolated panic attack. This was her reality. Loud noises in crowds would always do this. Maybe not every time, maybe less as the years passed, but it was always there in the background as a threatening presence.

And Gabe—Gabe had his own issues to deal with. She would just drag him down.

Laura looked at him as they joined the taxi queue. Those gentle eyes and the set of his jaw made her heart ache with emotion—and, yes, it was love. She'd tried lying to herself, but it was too strong and too deep to deny. But the hardest thing about love was putting that person first, knowing it would break your own heart. Gabe was scanning the crowd with that vigilant cop's eye, cataloging potential threats that probably weren't there. He was as broken as she was.

The thought made her want to cry, but she tamped it down. That was her specialty now.

Gabe guided her to the side, out of the flow, by a wall. "Where are you—"

"Upper West Side," she said quickly. "You?"

"Soho." Same city. Different worlds. Close enough to find each other. Far enough that they wouldn't run into each other by chance.

"Laura—" His hand moved toward his pocket, where he kept his phone, but he stopped.

She watched his hand, understood. Her own phone was right there in her bag.

"As much as I wish it could, it wouldn't work."

She whispered, "I know." Tears welled up in her eyes.

He nodded.

As they walked toward the taxi stand, he sought her hand with his and held it. She wanted to memorize the feel of his hand and his warmth beside her. Most of all, she wanted to believe it could work.

"There you are!" Kylie materialized beside them, coffee in hand. "Oh my gosh, this was so meant to be, meeting you two! The universe is just—" She made an explosion gesture with her hands.

A taxi pulled up.

"You take this one," Gabe said to Laura. "I'm in the opposite direction."

She nodded, and in that instant, he saw everything in her eyes—understanding, relief, and heartbreak all at once. Their hands touched, just for a second, as he helped her with her bag.

"Take care of yourself, Laura."

"You too."

He kissed her on the cheek and closed the door. Through the rear window, she took one last look at him standing on the curb, and then the taxi merged into traffic and was gone.

THE NEXT TAXI PULLED UP, and Gabe got in.

"Nice meeting you!" Kylie called after him as he climbed into the next cab.

As the taxi pulled away from the curb, Gabe stared out the window and recalled the look on Laura's face as they said goodbye. Carter's words echoed in his mind. "When you know, you know." And Gabe did. He knew it could never have worked. Some things could only survive in the space between real life and wishes, where trains made unscheduled stops on Christmas Eve.

CHAPTER ELEVEN

One Year Later

The therapist's office was deliberately neutral—beige walls, gray carpet, and a white noise machine that created a cocoon of privacy from the Upper West Side world outside its doors. Laura sat forward on the couch, actually smiling for the first time in one of these sessions.

"Six months without a panic attack," Dr. Pavar said, making a note in her folder. "That's real progress, Laura."

"It does feel like progress. I even walked past the Union Square holiday market last week. I didn't go in, but I walked past."

Her therapist set down her pen, choosing her words with the careful precision Laura had come to appreciate. Dr. Pavar leaned back in her chair, thoughtfully studying Laura. "We've talked about the trauma from Bryant Park, but there's something else we haven't fully explored. The man on the train—Gabe. You spent three days with him, became intimate with him, and then you parted without exchanging contact information."

Laura's chest tightened. "I know."

"Can you help me understand why? Not the circumstances—I understand you were both traumatized, both grieving. But in that moment, when you were saying goodbye, what stopped you from asking for his number?"

Laura was quiet for a long moment, watching snow fall past the window. "I thought... I thought I was protecting him."

"From?"

"From me." The words came out barely above a whisper. "I was still such a mess, Dr. Pavar. Still having panic attacks, still afraid of crowds and loud noises. I could barely take care of myself. How could I ask him to take on all of that?"

"And you believed he couldn't make that choice for himself?"

"I believed he deserved better than someone who couldn't even get through a train station without falling apart." Laura touched the wire angel in her pocket, the one she'd carried every day since. "He'd just lost his career, his identity. His hand was damaged. He was dealing with so much. Adding my mess to his seemed... cruel."

"Did he seem to think you were a burden?"

"No. But—" Laura stopped. "He wouldn't have. That's who he is. He would have taken on my brokenness because he's good and kind and protective. And I didn't want to be one more thing he had to protect."

"So you made the choice for him."

The words landed like a stone. "Yes."

"And how has that worked out?"

Laura laughed, but it was bitter. "I've spent a year searching for him. Doing internet searches, going back to places I thought he might be, and carrying this angel he gave me. It's just a holiday market trinket, but it's the only connection to him I have left."

Dr. Pavar was quiet for a moment. "What would you say to him now, if you could?"

"I'd say..." Laura's throat tightened. "I'd say I was wrong. That I should have trusted him to know what he wanted. That being broken together might have been better than being whole and alone."

The thought settled, then Dr. Pavar shifted her position in her chair in that way that usually signaled that their time was nearly up. "Well, the holidays are here. Maybe it's time to try experiencing some Christmas traditions again."

"Like what?"

"Take it slowly. Start small. You don't have to conquer everything at once. What's something you used to love about Christmas in the city?"

Laura thought of the tree at Rockefeller Center, the ice skating rink, and the window displays on Fifth Avenue. All of it was tangled up with before and after, with who she'd been and who she was now.

"I'll think about it," she said.

Outside, the December air was sharp enough to make her eyes water. She'd planned to go straight home, grade some papers, and eat leftover Thai food from last night. But her feet carried her east instead, toward the crowds she'd been avoiding for a year.

Rockefeller Center was exactly as overwhelming as she'd expected. Tourists everywhere, their voices a chorus of excitement and exhaustion. The tree towered above it all, looking magnificent. She forced herself to walk to the skating rink's edge, where she gripped the rail.

A couple was on the ice below. The woman wobbled on rental skates, laughing as she grabbed for her partner's arm. He caught her easily, pulled her upright, and kept his hand on her waist as they moved slowly around the rink.

The woman laughed and said something too far away to hear.

Then the man drew her closer and said something into her ear. Whatever it was drew a smile.

A memory washed over her like a wave. Gabe's steady hands on her waist. The way he'd caught her every time she fell. His voice warm against her ear: You're getting it. You're doing it.

The wire angel in her coat pocket pressed against her palm. She'd carried it every day for a year, unable to put it on this year's tree because that wouldn't be close enough.

She thought of his face in the gazebo, snowflakes caught in his dark hair. The way he'd whispered "Laura" in the darkness of her room. The way he'd looked at her in the morning light as if she was something precious he'd already lost. He'd made her heart feel so full, but that space was now empty.

I should never have let him go. If only...

The thought arrived fully formed, absolute.

She turned from the rink and walked home with sudden purpose, her mind already calculating. The train schedule, what to pack, and the time she would need to leave.

In her apartment, she pulled out her suitcase—the same one from last year—and opened her laptop. The Amtrak schedule loaded. December twenty-fourth. The 7:45 to Boston. Same departure time as before.

Christmas Eve. The train stopped only on Christmas Eve. That's what Mrs. Wright told them. If that was true, if whatever Christmas magic had brought them together was real, it could happen again under the same conditions.

She booked business class. The same seat wasn't available, but it was close enough.

GABE ARRIVED at Tom and Monica's Brooklyn brownstone already regretting his decision to come. But his friend had been persistent, and after a year of declining invitations, even Gabe recognized he couldn't keep saying no.

"Just dinner," Tom had promised. "Nothing fancy."

Tom opened the door, and Gabe walked inside.

As Gabe shrugged out of his jacket, Tom said, "Monica's made too much food, as usual."

They walked into the great room, where the table was set for four.

"Who else is coming?" Gabe asked.

"Oh, just a friend of Monica's," Tom said, too casually. "She's great. You'll like her."

Before Gabe could make an excuse to escape, Monica emerged from the kitchen with another woman behind her. For one heart-stopping moment, all he could see was the woman's hair—caramel-colored with waves falling just past her shoulders like—

She turned to reveal a perfectly nice face and the perfectly wrong person.

"Gabe, this is Susan," Monica said brightly. "Susan, Gabe."

Susan smiled and extended her hand. She had green eyes, not hazel. Her smile was wider, and her laugh came easier. Everything about her was just different enough to make the similarities painful.

They made it through appetizers with small talk about the weather, the city, and the impossible crowds of holiday tourists who managed to span the whole width of the sidewalk when walking together. Susan was a physical therapist, recently divorced, trying to rebuild her life. She was nice, interested, and not Laura.

During the main course, Susan noticed his hand. "Old injury?" she asked gently, with professional interest.

"Something like that."

Monica jumped in before he could deflect further. "He's being modest. He's a hero, actually. He saved people at that Christmas market shooting a couple of years ago."

Susan's eyes went wide. "Oh my gosh! That was

you? I remember reading about it. That must have been terrifying! How did you—"

"Excuse me."

Gabe pushed back from the table and walked to the bathroom with measured steps. After turning the door lock, he gripped the edge of the sink until his knuckles went white. The face in the mirror looked hollow and haunted—a ghost of a man going through the motions of living.

He couldn't do this. He couldn't sit at that table and pretend to be someone capable of moving forward. He couldn't listen to Susan's perfectly reasonable interest in his story when the only person he wanted to tell it to had disappeared in a taxi a year ago.

He splashed cold water on his face, dried his hands, and returned to the dining room.

"I'm sorry," he said, not sitting back down. "I'm not feeling well."

Monica started to protest, but Tom put a hand on her arm.

To Susan, Gabe managed, "It was lovely meeting you."

She nodded kindly. "You too."

Tom followed him to the door. "Gabe, come on. Give her a chance."

"It's not about her."

"Then what?"

"Thanks for dinner."

He walked out into the December night. Families were gathered inside their warm homes. He walked without destination until a sports bar's neon sign promised nothing more complicated than beer and games on TV.

Inside, the Knicks were losing on three different screens. He took a seat at the bar, ordered a beer, and tried to lose himself in the game. On one screen, an old Christmas movie played with closed captions, but nobody seemed to be watching.

Two guys next to him were arguing about the referee's call when one guy's phone rang.

"Yeah, I'm at Murphy's. No, I told you I'm not doing Christmas Eve at your sister's. Because last year was a disaster! No, that's not... Fine. FINE! You know what? Whatever. Okay, I'll be there."

He hung up. His friend laughed. "Whipped."

"Shut up. You don't get it. She almost left me last year."

"Over Christmas dinner?"

"Over me being a stubborn butthole who couldn't admit I was wrong." He put on his jacket while his friend signaled for another beer. "My dad was married three times. You know why? He never learned when to stop being right and to start being happy."

"Deep thoughts from Jack Daniels."

"Screw you. I'm serious. Sometimes you get one shot at not mucking up your whole life. One shot at the person who actually gets you. And if you're too stupid or too proud to take it..." He shrugged. "You end up like my dad. Seventy years old, spending Christmas with wife number three."

The friend was quiet for a moment. "So you're going to her sister's."

With a nod, he said, "Yes. I'm going to her sister's. I'm gonna eat her mother's dry turkey, and I'm gonna smile at my brother-in-law's stupid jokes. Because she's worth it."

"That's a goddamn Christmas miracle right there."

"What, me being a decent person?"

"No, you're finding someone—anyone."

"Shut up."

Gabe left money on the bar and walked out.

Christmas miracle. Mrs. Wright's knowing smile flashed in his mind as she told them, "Christmas Eve is special. On Christmas Eve, the train stops for people who need to find something they've lost—or someone. Sometimes it's both."

Christmas Eve was special. He walked home with sudden purpose. Once there, he pulled up the Amtrak schedule on his phone. December twenty-fourth, the 7:45 p.m. to Boston. The exact train from last year.

Same date, same time, same route. If Evergreen Junction existed—if it appeared for people who needed it—then he still needed it. He needed Laura.

Coach seats were the only ones left. He booked a seat anyway.

LAURA

Laura lay in bed watching the clock tick toward morning. She'd packed and repacked three times, trying to decide what to wear to possibly see the love of her life again after a year of silence. Finally, she settled on the same clothes from before—jeans, a cream sweater, and a gray coat. The wire angel went in the pocket, its edges familiar against her palm.

GABE

Ninety blocks south, Gabe sat by his window watching the city sleep. His duffel bag waited by the door, packed with enough clothes for a couple of days. His soft-shell jacket hung on the doorknob—the one he'd worn that first night.

LAURA

At 5:30 p.m., Laura went to the subway. The express wasn't running, so she got on the local and stared at her watch. Minutes passed as she tried not to think about what she was doing. Hope was dangerous. Hope could break you. But not hoping had already broken her slowly over the course of a year.

GABE

At 5:45 p.m., Gabe walked to the subway. The train was already crowded with rush hour and last-minute Christmas Eve shoppers. He stood near the door, checking his watch every thirty seconds.

He entered Penn Station, where the main concourse was even more frenetic than the usual rush hour, with commuters and holiday travelers. Families with too much luggage, couples arguing over which platform was theirs, and solo travelers walking with purpose toward their trains.

LAURA

Once in Penn Station, Laura stopped at the departure board. Track 12. She had twenty minutes. Heading straight for her platform, she passed the coffee kiosk where a year ago Kylie had stopped for her latte. A man stood there with his back to her—tall, dark-haired, with broad shoulders held just the same way. She stepped toward him.

He turned. Not Gabe. Never Gabe.

She kept walking.

GABE

Gabe reached the platform early and found his car near the back of the train. He knew the moment he sat down that this was going to be a rough trip. The seat was too narrow, the man beside him was already spreading into his space, and the family behind him was preparing for what would clearly be a long journey with an overtired toddler.

But it was coach or nothing. So here he sat, several cars back from where he wanted to be, seated on the opposite side of the platform with a view of the wall through his window. When his view wasn't blocked by fellow passengers, he caught sight of people outside walking toward the business class seats up ahead. Once, he thought he saw someone in a gray coat, but a man boarded and paused in the aisle, blocking his view.

Around him, families negotiated who would sit where, couples settled in for the journey, and solo travelers claimed window seats. The car was filling up fast.

LAURA

Toward the front of the train, Laura sat down in her reserved seat, two rows back from where it had all started. She placed her messenger bag on her lap—that small barrier against the world—and watched the platform through the window.

"Hello."

Laura smiled as an elderly woman stowed her bag in the overhead rack and then settled down in the seat beside her. She busied herself rustling gift bags and adjusting her coat, and then turned to Laura. "Going home for Christmas?"

Laura thought about how to answer that. "Something like that."

The train began to slide away from the lights of Penn Station into the darkness of the tunnel. When it emerged above ground, it was nearly as dark. Her heart beat a steady cadence along with the train as she wished it to stop at Evergreen Junction. *Please stop. Please stop. Please stop.*

GABE

In coach class, Gabe sat rigid in his seat, hands clenched on his thighs. Through the window, New York fell away, and the suburbs began to replace high-rise apartments. Every mile that passed felt like a countdown.

LAURA

Stamford came and went. Laura remembered how Gabe had come to her aid there. That was where it all started.

By the time they left New Haven, snow dusted the rooftops as they rolled along through Connecticut. Laura pressed her face to the window, searching for any sign of the impossible—of a depot that shouldn't exist, of a town that appeared only when needed.

Trees pressed close to the tracks while snow weighed down the branches. Last year, it had looked just like this, and they were nearing the place where they'd slowed down before.

But the train didn't change. It didn't slow down. It didn't stop.

It was gone. They'd long since passed through the place where Evergreen Junction should have been. There was nothing but flying snow and the steady clack of wheels on rails carrying them forward.

Laura's heart sank. Beside her, the elderly woman asked if she was alright. Did she need water? Laura shook her head, unable to speak past the grief crushing her throat.

GABE

He'd timed it enough to determine that halfway between New Haven and New London, the magic was supposed to happen. Unable to stand anymore, with the businessman snoring beside him and a toddler fussing behind him, Gabe had moved. He stood and made his way to the café car for a better view.

Twenty minutes out of New Haven, he started to recognize things. Or thought he did. That curve in the tracks, the way the forest opened slightly then closed again. Twenty-three minutes. Twenty-four.

There—those pines. He was sure of it. The exact configuration he'd memorized, three tall ones with a smaller one leaning. He pressed closer to the door window, one hand on the handle to steady himself as the train rocked.

Twenty-six minutes.

Nothing. They were past it already, the forest unchanging, no sign of a depot or a town or anything but Connecticut wilderness.

He couldn't breathe, so he made his way to the space between cars, where the cold hit him immediately through the gaps in the rubber housing between cars. Wind whistled through, carrying the smell of snow. He had missed Evergreen Junction. The train hadn't stopped.

Something died in his chest. He'd been a fool to think magic could happen again. Only a fool could believe in Christmas miracles, impossible towns, and second chances.

"Sir?"

He turned to find a conductor behind him, looking disapproving.

"Sir, passengers aren't permitted to ride here. You need to return to your seat."

"I was just—"

"Federal railroad regulations, sir. You can pass through to move between cars, but you can't remain here. Please return to your seat immediately."

Gabe wanted to argue, wanted to explain that he was looking for something impossible, that he'd already missed it, that it didn't matter anymore. Instead, he nodded and walked back to his seat, where the businessman had expanded further into his space, and the toddler behind him kept kicking his seat.

The train rolled on, carrying him away from the life he had hoped for, away from the one chance at love he'd passed up.

CHAPTER TWELVE

GABE

THE REST of the journey to the next stop, New London, was a fog of disappointment so thick it felt lodged in his throat. When the train finally pulled into the station, Gabe was among the first out, needing to escape the confined space and shed the weight of his foolish hope.

Once inside the station, he found the ticket window and confirmed what he already knew from checking the schedule on his phone. The next train back to New York wasn't for another ninety minutes. He had ninety minutes to kill in a station with nothing but benches and vending machines. So he ventured outside and found a bar across the street, the perfect place to wait for the next train in misery.

LAURA

Laura had been in the bathroom for twenty minutes when someone knocked on the stall door to ask if she was all right. She'd managed to say yes, she was fine; she just needed a moment—a moment to wipe her red eyes and nose with toilet paper so thick it seemed to dissolve in her hands.

She pulled herself together enough to go straight to the sink and splash cold water on her face, but it wasn't enough to erase the heartbreak that seemed to be written all over it. Her reflection looked hollow with red-rimmed eyes and a washed-out complexion, which was just about right. It was the expression of someone who had gambled everything on Christmas magic and lost.

She returned to the waiting area, found a bench facing the tracks, and sat down. Her crying jag in the bathroom had shortened the wait for her return trip to New York. *You can do this. You've got to.* She just had to sit here and not fall apart for a little over an hour. Then the train ride would be simple enough. She would close her eyes and pretend to be sleeping while dying inside. From Penn Station, she'd splurge on a taxi. Before long, she'd be inside her apartment, where she could cry undisturbed and learn not to believe in impossible things.

Around her, the station carried on with its mundane business. A custodian pushed a mop bucket across the floor. A couple quietly argued about missed connections. And footsteps echoed in the large, open space.

She pulled out her book and stared at the same page.

GABE

The bar was exactly what Gabe had expected—dim lighting, sticky floors, and a bartender who didn't ask questions when someone ordered whiskey at eight-thirty on Christmas Eve. There were a few other patrons, all with the look of regulars who had nowhere better to be.

He sat at the far end of the bar, facing the door, and nursed his drink. Forty-five minutes until he'd head back. Forty-five minutes to watch his hope die.

The whiskey burned, but not enough to cauterize the wound of knowing he'd never see Laura again. He'd had an entire year to kick himself for letting her walk away without fighting for her. But that didn't stop him from wallowing in more self-loathing.

"Rough night?" the bartender asked, refilling without being asked.

"Rough year," Gabe replied.

"I hear that." The bartender moved on to other customers, leaving Gabe alone with his regrets.

After a while, he checked his watch. It was time to head back. He left cash on the bar and walked back through the cold to the station.

LAURA

Laura saw a tall man walk in through the street-side entrance, and her heart stopped. When would she stop seeing him in every tall man with dark hair? She turned back to her book, disgusted with herself for still looking and hoping even now.

The waiting room had filled with people heading back to New York. She kept her head down so she wouldn't make eye contact with anyone and then have to pretend that she was okay.

When the train pulled into the station, she stood and went out to the platform with everyone else. The train back to New York was even more crowded with people heading home to their families for Christmas or spending the holidays in the city. She found her window seat, clutched her messenger bag, and turned toward the darkness outside her window.

GABE

Gabe arrived just as the train pulled into the station. His coach car was packed, but he'd managed to reserve a window seat near the back where he could stare at the passing lights and houses in peace. There was no need to time anything or to watch for landmarks. Before long, he just sat with his eyes closed and tried not to think about a woman in a gray coat and the way her hand had felt in his when they'd walked through the snow.

They passed through the place where Evergreen Junction should have been without him even noticing.

LAURA

The return train was full. Laura settled into her window seat and leaned her head back. She'd been so certain. Same day, same time, same desperate need. Mrs. Wright's words had seemed like a promise: "On Christmas Eve, the train stops for people who need to find something they've lost—or someone. Sometimes it's both."

But maybe that was the problem. Maybe she'd passed up her one chance to be happy, and this was a message that some things couldn't be fixed. She'd had their one chance, and she'd lost it. Some losses were permanent.

Through the window, Connecticut rolled past in the darkness—invisible towns, invisible lives, and an invisible depot that held everything she'd ever wanted and could never have.

Her phone sat dark in her lap. She'd typed his name into search engines so many times over the past year. She'd found police officers with similar names, none of them him. She'd read every news article she could find about the Bryant Park shooting, but none contained even a clue about how to find him.

She touched the wire angel in her pocket, the one he'd bought her at the market. Its edges had worn smooth from a year of carrying it everywhere. "I'm sorry," she thought, although she didn't know if she was apologizing to him or to herself. "I'm so sorry I let you go."

The train's rhythm was hypnotic. The same wheels

on the same tracks, now taking her away from a place she'd been happy.

The conductor's voice crackled over the intercom: "Penn Station, next stop. New York Penn Station."

Laura gathered her bag, pulled on her coat, and wrapped her cream-colored scarf around her neck. The train slowed to a stop, and Laura joined the other passengers crowding the aisle to wait for the doors to open.

GABE

The coach car smelled like stale coffee. Gabe leaned his shoulder against the window and pressed his hand to his thigh. The tremor was worse than it had been in months.

All he wanted right now was to go home and to stop wanting Laura. It was time to face the fact that he'd lost her.

His friend Tom was right. You didn't get a second chance at something like this. You got one shot at happiness, and if you were too scared or too stupid to take it, the world moved on without you.

His phone was dead. He'd forgotten his charger. He'd been distracted by his last-minute planning, not to mention his desperate belief that tonight would be different.

The dead phone didn't matter. He had no way to search for her, even if he knew how. There was no phone call or text that could reach across the vast distance between them.

An announcement cut through his thoughts: "Penn Station, next stop. New York Penn Station."

Gabe reached up and pulled his jacket down from the overhead rack. Around him, other passengers gathered their belongings as the train eased into the station. When the doors finally opened, he stepped onto the platform and walked toward the main concourse.

He'd almost reached the concourse when ahead of him, perhaps fifty feet away, he saw a woman in a gray coat. She walked with her head down and her shoulders raised just a bit, as if she might be tense.

Something about how she was walking and the particular set of her shoulders made his breath catch.

She turned slightly to avoid another passenger, and he caught a glimpse of her profile.

His heart stopped.

"Laura."

The word came out barely above a whisper, lost in the echoing space of the station. He walked faster, weaving his way through the crowd with his eyes locked on her. "Laura!"

LAURA

A voice cut through the white noise of the station like a physical force.

She knew that voice. She'd heard it whisper her name in darkness and laugh at her terrible skating. He'd told her she was brave when she felt like a coward.

But it couldn't be real. She was exhausted and grieving, and her mind was playing cruel tricks.

"Laura, please. Turn around."

That was closer this time. But it couldn't be real.

She turned.

Gabe stood ten feet away, looking exactly as wrecked as she felt. His hair was disheveled, and his eyes were red-rimmed and desperate.

"You're here," she whispered.

He took a step toward her, then stopped as if afraid she might disappear. "I went looking for you."

Her voice broke. "The train didn't stop."

"I know."

They stood frozen, neither quite believing the other was real. Other passengers flowed past them like water around stones, but Laura couldn't move or breathe or do anything but stare.

"I'm sorry," Gabe said, the words tumbling out. "For letting you go."

"I was scared," Laura interrupted. "I was too broken. I thought you deserved someone whole."

"I want *you*." He closed the distance between them in three strides. "Whole or broken, I want *you*. I've wanted you every single day for a year."

"I tried to find you," she said, tears streaming down her face now. "I went back to Bryant Park thinking maybe—"

"I drove to Connecticut." His hand came up to cup her face, trembling against her skin. "Looking for a town that doesn't exist. Looking for you."

"You found me," she managed through tears and laughter.

His thumb brushed away her tears. "For the love of God, give me your phone number."

She laughed and pulled out her phone. "You can have my number, my email, my address—"

"And you?" She'd barely managed a nod when he kissed her. Right there on the platform with travelers streaming past and announcements echoing overhead, he pulled her against him and kissed her like a man who'd been drowning and just broke through the surface.

She kissed him back as all the longing, grief, and desperate hope of the past year poured into this moment, this impossible, perfect moment.

When the kiss ended, they clung to each other as if letting go might mean losing one another. Gabe rested his forehead against hers.

"I'm still broken," he said quietly. "My hand isn't going to get better. I'm not the cop I used to be—"

"I haven't had a panic attack in six months," Laura interrupted. "But I still can't handle some crowds. I'm not—"

"That's okay." He pulled back to look at her. "We'll figure it out—if you'll have me."

A feeling of peace came over her, and she smiled and shrugged. "I love you. What else can I do?"

His smile transformed his face, erasing a year of grief in an instant. "You can love me as long as you'll have me because I love you, too."

He kissed her again, softer this time, as if sealing a promise.

Around them, Penn Station continued its late-night

rhythm with trains arriving and leaving, people coming and going, because life went on.

But for Laura and Gabe, the world had narrowed to this: two people who'd found one another again, who had learned the hard way that some gifts were fragile and worth fighting for.

"Come home with me," Gabe said, his arms still wrapped around her. "Or I can come to yours. I don't care. I just—I can't let you out of my sight again."

"They're both about the same distance from here. I don't care. Your place is fine," Laura said. "As long as we're together. Wait! Pull out your phone. Now. Let's not take any chances." He laughed, but the humor of it faded, and they quickly made sure they could reach one another.

When they'd finished exchanging contact information, Gabe slipped his phone into his pocket. His eyes sparkled. "Do you think that's enough? I'm thinking carrier pigeons."

Laura furrowed her eyebrows. "That's very Brando of you."

"Too much?" he asked.

She held back a laugh. "I mean, think of the upkeep. Although that's better than a tracking device."

His eyes brightened. "I hadn't thought of that. Genius!"

Laura wrinkled her face. "Gabe, we'll be fine."

"Yeah?" He pulled her closer. "So stalking each other is out of the question."

Laura grinned and nodded.

They stood together just holding each other while

the truth slowly sank in. As impossible as it seemed, in a city of eight million people, they'd found one another again.

A conductor walked by and said with a grin, "Don't you two have someplace better to go?"

Gabe laughed. "We do, as a matter of fact." He took Laura's hand, and they left the platform.

"Look." Laura pointed to the clock in Moynihan Train Hall. It was nearly midnight. "Merry Christmas," Laura whispered.

Gabe turned from the clock. "Merry Christmas." He kissed her, then wrapped his arms around her. "The first—no, the second of many—"

Suddenly serious, Laura said, "Gabe, it's the third."

The thought gripped him so, it was a moment before he could speak. "So it is. Merry Christmas."

Hand in hand, they walked out of Penn Station, leaving behind them the trains that had brought them together. In the darkness of the tunnel, the last Christmas Eve train pulled out of the station, carrying other passengers on an unscheduled journey to Evergreen Junction.

Meanwhile, Gabe and Laura's new journey was only beginning.

EPILOGUE

CHRISTMAS EVE, One Year Later

Laura drank a toast in the rustic wooden shelter at Central Park's Wagner Cove. The lake stretched beyond them, where the surface was beginning to freeze at the edges as snow fell and dissolved in the dark watery center.

When they'd said their goodbyes, Gabe took Laura's hand, leaving behind the clink of champagne glasses, and Tom and Monica's quiet laughter drifted from the small gathering they'd just left.

"Mrs. Lawson," Gabe said, just to hear it again.

"Mr. Lawson," she replied, squeezing his hand.

Her dress, a simple ivory tea-length silk, was mostly hidden beneath the winter white cashmere coat he'd helped her into moments ago. The coat had been his wedding gift to her, to replace the gray one she'd worn on the train. "For new memories," he'd said when she'd opened the box.

They followed a winding stone path through

winter-bare trees. A light coating of snow muffled their footsteps as the cove's hidden intimacy gave way gradually to the more open landscape of the park. Along a paved walkway dusted with white and lined with park benches, lampposts glowed in the gathering dusk. A short walk along Terrace Drive led to 72nd Street and Central Park West. There, Laura spotted a white horse-drawn carriage waiting at the park's edge. It was decorated with evergreen boughs and white roses that were already catching snowflakes. The horse stamped once, breath steaming in the cold air, and the bells on his harness jingled softly.

The driver, an older man in a top hat and formal coat, touched the brim of his hat. "Congratulations, Mr. and Mrs. Lawson."

Gabe helped Laura up the narrow step, and she settled into a red velvet seat. He tucked a thick blanket around them both, and the carriage lurched gently into motion.

They followed the park past trees white with snow, glowing streetlights, and the city skyline rising beyond. Laura felt as though she was in someone else's fairy tale.

GABE TURNED to look at his bride. Snowflakes had caught in her hair, which she'd worn drawn back simply. Her cheeks were pink from the cold, the champagne, and the joy. She'd never looked more beautiful.

She slipped her arm around his and rested her head on his shoulder. Her hand with its simple gold band rested on his, with its matching gold band. Inside was inscribed, "Stay with me."

The horse's pace was steady but unhurried, as if they had all the time in the world. Which, she supposed, they did now.

"Laura Lawson," she said, trying it out. "I could have kept Quinn, but..."

"But?"

"But I'm not the woman I was on the first day I met you. The woman I've become deserves a new name."

"You saved me that day."

"We saved each other. It just took us a while to realize it."

As they neared 59th Street, city lights twinkled with thousands of windows lit up for Christmas Eve. South of those lights was their apartment in Chelsea, the one they'd chosen together in June, with two bedrooms because, as he'd told Laura, hope was a good thing to have.

"Next Christmas," Laura said, "we should take a train somewhere and just see where it goes."

"It'll just be a regular train."

"I know. That's why we should take it. To prove we don't need enchanted holiday towns anymore."

"We never did," Gabe said. "We just needed to be brave enough to choose one another."

The snow was falling harder now, in fat flakes that seemed to glow in the streetlights. The driver pulled over across from the park, where they would return to the city with all its noise, complications, and beautiful, ordinary life.

"Tell me something," Laura said. "If you could go back to that first night on the train, knowing everything that would happen—the panic attacks, the separation, the year of agonized searching—would you still get off at that depot?"

Gabe didn't hesitate. "Every time."

"Even knowing the town might disappear? That we would have to find each other the hard way?"

"Especially then." He turned her face toward his. "The hard way is the only way that counts."

She kissed him then, in the carriage with snow falling and Central Park sliding past like a dream.

"READY?" the driver called back.

Laura looked at Gabe. Her husband. The man she'd saved and who'd saved her right back. The stranger on a train who'd become everything.

"Ready," they said together.

The carriage pulled over and parked on Central Park South. They were back to the real world, where love was harder and messier, and all the more perfect for it.

With the park behind them, the city lights beckoned, promising a future of ordinary mornings, quiet evenings, and the small daily magic of building a life. As they walked away, the bells on the horse's harness jingled one last time like the last notes of a carol about miracles that sometimes come true.

THANK YOU!

THANK YOU FOR READING! If you enjoyed this book, please consider leaving a review or a rating. Your feedback on bookstore, Goodreads, and Bookbub websites helps other readers discover books they'll enjoy.

BOOK NEWS

Sign up for the J.L. Jarvis Journal for exclusive benefits, including free books, special offers, exclusive content, and updates on new releases: news.jljarvis.com

DISCUSSION QUESTIONS

The Magic of Evergreen Junction

1. What do you think Evergreen Junction represents in the story? Have you ever experienced a place that felt "outside of time" or magical during the holidays? If you could, what would you want it to be like?

2. Mrs. Wright tells Laura and Gabe that "the train stops for people who need to find something they've lost—or someone." What do you think each character needed to find beyond each other?

3. The town only appears on Christmas Eve for those who need it. If you could visit Evergreen Junction, what would you hope to find there?

Romance and Connection

4. Laura and Gabe maintain their distance from each other initially, despite their obvious connection. What do you think finally allowed them to drop their walls and connect?

5. The skating scene is a turning point in their relationship. What was it about the activity that helped them deepen their bond?

6. Discuss the moment when Gabe and Laura realize who each other is. How does their shared past both complicate and strengthen their connection?

Christmas Traditions and Symbolism

7. The wire angel plays an important symbolic role throughout the story. What does it represent for Laura, and how does its meaning evolve?

8. The story features several Christmas traditions—caroling, markets, church services, ice skating. Which scene felt most magical to you, and why?

9. Mae's bookshop combines books, tea, and community. What role do gathering places like this play in the holiday season?

. . .

Choices and Second Chances

10. Both Laura and Gabe initially choose to part ways without exchanging contact information. Do you think this was the right decision at that moment? Why or why not?

11. A year later, they both return to the same train on Christmas Eve, hoping to magically find one another. What does this say about hope and taking chances?

12. The story ends with them choosing an ordinary life together over magical intervention. How is this significant for them?

Character Growth

13. How does Laura change from the beginning of the story to the end? What moments show her becoming braver?

14. Gabe struggles with his identity after losing his career. How does his time in Evergreen Junction help him discover who he is beyond his job?

15. Both characters learn to accept their vulnerabilities. What does the story suggest

about the relationship between
vulnerability and love?

COMMUNITY AND CONNECTION

16. The townspeople of Evergreen Junction—
    Mae, Mrs. Wright, the carolers, and the
    vendors—all contribute to Laura and Gabe's
    journey. How does community play a role
    in healing and happiness?
17. Compare the anonymous crowds of Penn
    Station with the intimate community of
    Evergreen Junction. What does the story
    suggest about the importance of human
    connection?

THE JOURNEY MOTIF

18. Trains are central to the story—both literal
    and metaphorical. What does the train
    journey represent for Laura and Gabe?
19. The story begins with "trains carry two
    kinds of travelers: those rushing toward
    holiday celebrations and those quietly
    slipping away from them." Which category
    do Laura and Gabe fall into, and how does
    this change?

20. In the epilogue, Laura suggests they should take a train "just to see where it goes" and prove "we don't need magic towns anymore." What does this tell us about how they've grown?

LOOKING Deeper

21. Carter and Kylie serve as a contrast to Laura and Gabe—openly enthusiastic about their love versus quietly guarded. How did their presence affect the way Laura and Gabe parted? Would Kylie and Carter's absence have changed anything?

22. Discuss the role of fate versus choice in the story. Are Laura and Gabe fated to be together, or do they choose each other?

JUST FOR FUN!

23. If *A Christmas Eve Stop* were adapted into a movie, who would you cast as Laura and Gabe?

24. Which scene would you most look forward to seeing—the bookshop, the ice skating, the Christmas market, or the church service?

25. If you were to escape to create your ideal Christmas in your ideal place, where would it be, and what would it look like?

26. If you could have dinner at one location in Evergreen Junction, would you choose Mae's cozy bookshop, the inn's delicious dining room, or some pub grub at the tavern?

Merry Christmas, and happy reading!

ABOUT THE AUTHOR

J.L. Jarvis is a left-handed former opera singer/teacher/lawyer who writes books. She now lives and writes on a mountaintop in upstate New York.

jljarvis.com